READING

Comprehension • Spelling • Grammar • Review

Contents

Week 19

Week 20

Week 21

Week 22

Week 23

Week 24

Week 25

Week 26

Week 27

REVIEW 3

Week 28

Week 29

Week 30

Week 31

Week 32

Week 33

Week 34

Week 35

Week 36

REVIEW 4

Year Planner

	Week 1	Week 2	Week 3	Week 4	Week 5	Week 6	Week 7	Week 8	Week 9
Comprehension	Think marks	Finding facts and information	Making inferences	Finding the main idea	Finding the main idea	Finding facts and information	Compare and contrast	Finding the main idea	Sequencing events
Spelling	Verb endings: s, es	Digraphs: ar, or	Endings: y, ey	scr, spr, str	Digraph: qu	Suffixes: ing, ed	Prefix: un	Digraph: oo	Soft c
Grammar	Common nouns	Collective nouns	Proper nouns	Personal pronouns	Articles and nouns	Punctuating sentences	Adjectives	Irregular plurals	Commas in lists
Review	Spelling			Grammar			Comprehension		

	Week 10	Week 11	Week 12	Week 13	Week 14	Week 15	Week 16	Week 17	Week 18
Comprehension	Making inferences	Visualisation	Finding the main idea	Visualisation	Sequencing events	Compare and contrast	Compare and contrast	Making connections	Word study
Spelling	Plurals with y	The j sound	Endings: le, el, al	Digraph: wh	Exceptions	Plurals: s, ves	Long oo exceptions	Suffixes: ful, less	Silent letters
Grammar	Action verbs	Present tense	Full stops and question marks	Relating verbs	Past tense	Helping verbs	Future tense	Verb groups	Full stops and exclamation marks
Review	Spelling			Grammar			Comprehension		

	Week 19	Week 20	Week 21	Week 22	Week 23	Week 24	Week 25	Week 26	Week 27
Comprehension	Think marks	Making inferences	Visualisation	Finding the main idea	Finding the main idea	Sequencing events	Finding facts and information	Compare and contrast	Making inferences
Spelling	Suffixes: er, est	Homophones	Suffixes: ing, ed	The k sound: k, ck	Suffix: ly	Endings: dge, ge	Compound words	Contractions	Plurals: s, es
Grammar	Possessive nouns	Possessive pronouns	Saying verbs	Direct speech	Questions and exclamations	Sequencing adverbs	Noun groups	Conjunctions	Contractions
Review	Spelling			Grammar			Comprehension		

	Week 28	Week 29	Week 30	Week 31	Week 32	Week 33	Week 34	Week 35	Week 36
Comprehension	Drawing conclusions	Making predictions	Visualisation	Finding the main idea	Visualisation	Compare and contrast	Sequencing events	Compare and contrast	Making inferences
Spelling	Irregular past tense verbs	Split digraphs	Digraphs: ea, ee	Endings: ar, er, or	Digraphs: ai, a–e	Word building	Suffixes: er, est	Tricky words	Suffixes: ment, ness
Grammar	Irregular past tense verbs	Prepositions	Adverb groups	Simple sentences	Punctuate simple sentences	Compound sentences	Capitalising proper nouns	Expanding sentences	Formal and informal language
Review	Spelling			Grammar			Comprehension		

Go, Go Gecko

Think marks

To help you understand what you are reading, you can use **special marks**. These help you see the parts you understand and any new vocabulary.

I can see this part

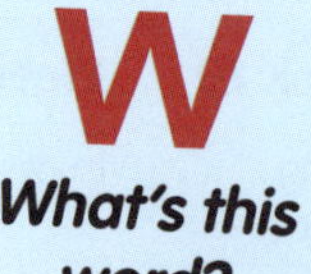

What's this word?

I understand this part

Read the passage.

Use 👀 for parts of the story you can see.

Use a W for words you didn't know the meaning of.

Place a ✓ next to the part of the story you understand.

The Chalk Box

The chalk box moves! The class gasps. Just a tiny gasp each but together it makes the sound of a gust of wind.

Mr Mooney turns around. We're sitting quietly so there's nothing he can say.

Mr Mooney turns back to the board. We go back to staring at the chalk box.

Circle the correct answer.

1. **What** are the children watching?
   a Mr Mooney b chalk box c gust of wind d board
2. **Who** is sitting quietly?
   a the class b the gecko c Mr Mooney d the principal
3. **What** is moving?
   a the chalk box b the wind c the board d the class
4. **What** is a *gasp*?
   a the sound of the wind b a quick intake of breath
5. Which word could replace *turns* in this story?
   a spins b pushes c circles d shows

Go, Go Gecko

Read the whole story

Read the passage.

Use Think Marks to help you understand the passage.

Box **what** Mr Mooney's face looks like.

Underline **where** the gecko climbs.

A Gecko on the Teacher!

The gecko jumps onto Mr Mooney's hand. It runs up his arm. It leaps onto his head and waves at us.

Mr Mooney's eyes roll up and his mouth is the shape of an O.

His arms freeze halfway to his head, as if he's too afraid to move.

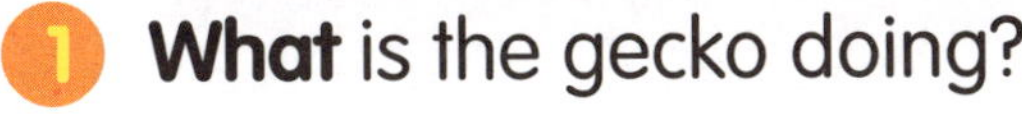

1. **What** is the gecko doing?

2. **How** does Mr Mooney feel?

3. Write about a time when you were really surprised by something.

Week 1 Day 3 Spelling

Verb endings: s, es

The **suffix s** can be added to a verb to make it agree with its subject; e.g., Trees grow. A tree grow**s**. If the verb ends in **s**, **sh**, **ch**, **x** or **z**, add **es**; e.g., The bees buzz. The bee buzz**es**.

1 Copy each list word.

chops ________	melts ________	dances ________
bites ________	hammers ________	listens ________
bumps ________	crosses ________	blesses ________
fixes ________	breaks ________	munches ________
grows ________	buys ________	pushes ________
chases ________	behaves ________	coaches ________
hurts ________	covers ________	

2 Underline the spelling mistake. Write the word correctly.

a She dancess to the music. ________

b He listenes to the radio. ________

c Mario breakes the stick in half. ________

d Dad buyes food at the shops. ________

3 Unscramble the letters to make a list word.

a ssescro ________ **b** versco ________

c ltsme ________ **d** havesbe ________

e chescoa ________ **f** ersmham ________

4 Write the name for each.

a m ________

b d ________

c b ________

Verb endings: s, es

1 **Turn each word into a list word.**

chop	chops
break	
push	

bite	
grow	

Challenge words

2 **Copy each challenge word.**

polishes ____________ finishes ____________

vanishes ____________ switches ____________

touches ____________ attaches ____________

launches ____________ measures ____________

teaches ____________ guesses ____________

3 **Use as many challenge words as possible to make a silly story.**

4 **Colour the correct word to complete each sentence.**

a Dad always [finishes] [finish] his dinner before me.

b The carpenter [measure] [measures] each piece of wood.

c The rain [vanishes] [vanish] when the sun comes out.

d Jack [teach] [teaches] his dog how to fetch.

e Before going to bed, Dad [switches] [switch] off all the lights.

Common nouns

A **noun** names a person, place, animal or thing. A **common noun** names a general person, place, animal or thing; e.g., girl, park, dog, cup.

1 Draw lines to match the noun to the picture.

a

b 

c

d 

e 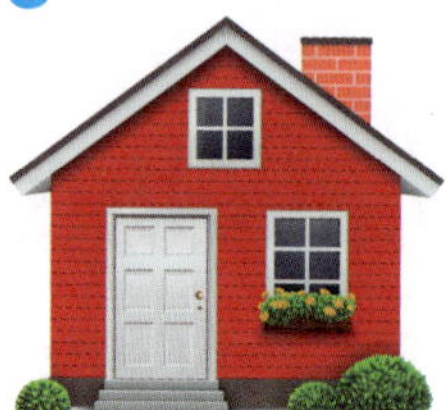

cyclist sun house hat pig

2 Draw lines to match the columns.

a bus	place
b baby	animal
c monkey	thing
d museum	person

3 Label the pictures.

a 

____

b 

____

4 Use the letters in the circle to make a noun.

a 

____

b 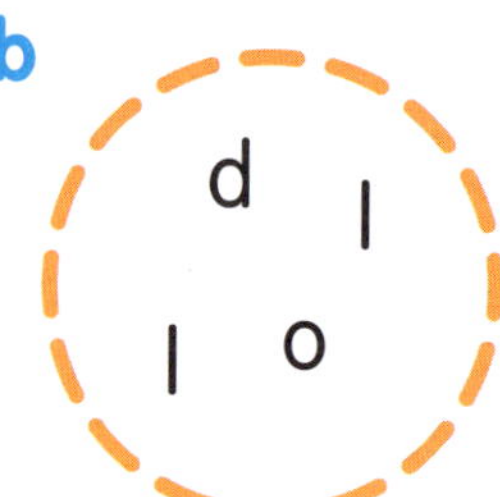

____

Week 2 Day 1 Comprehension

Tim's Money Tree

Finding facts and information

To find facts and information in a text, ask the questions **Who? What? Where?** or **When?** The answers can be clearly seen in the text.

Read the passage.

Box **what** the flowers grow into.

Circle **who** is asking about a tree.

A Good Idea

"Haven't you ever seen a money tree?" asked Mandy.

Tim shook his head. "How do people get a money tree?"

"Easy!" Mandy laughed. "They plant a coin in a pot full of dirt. Then they water it."

"When the coin grows into a tree, flowers grow on it. The flowers turn into money," she told him.

Underline **what** type of tree Tim is asking about.

Colour **where** to plant the coin.

Circle the correct answer.

1. **Who** is explaining the money tree?
   - a Mandy
   - b Tim
   - c Mum
   - d Sam

2. **What** is the first step to grow a money tree?
   - a Prune the tree.
   - b Plant a coin.
   - c Water the plant.
   - d Pick the flowers.

3. **Where** do you grow a money tree?
   - a in the forest
   - b next to a bank
   - c in a pot
   - d by a lake

Tim's Money Tree

Read the passage.

Circle who was playing tricks.

Box what Mandy needed to do.

Underline what Mandy wanted to buy.

Trouble!

Mum didn't like Mandy playing tricks on Tim.

"There's only one thing to do," Mum said. "Take the coins out of your piggybank and stick them on Tim's tree."

"But I was saving up to buy a book!" Mandy told her.

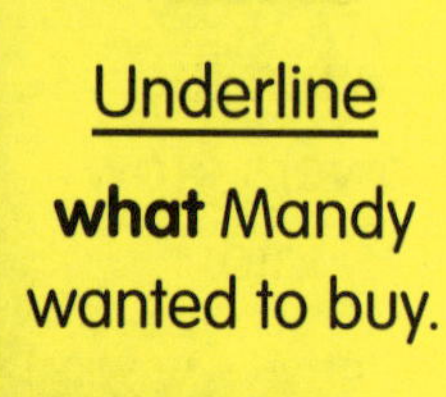

1. **Who** was playing tricks? ______________________
2. **What** does Mum want Mandy to do? ______________________
   ____
3. **Why** must Mandy do this? ______________________
   ____
4. **What** had Mandy been saving for? ______________________

Digraphs: ar, or

Two letters that make a single sound are called a **digraph**. The letters **ar** can make the **single sound ar**; e.g., st**ar** or the **single sound or**; e.g., w**ar**.

The letters **or** can make the **single sound or**; e.g., b**or**n or the **single sound er**; e.g., w**or**m.

1 Copy each list word.

arm ________	ward ________	wart ________
war ________	warn ________	warp ________
car ________	born ________	apart ________
worm ________	storm ________	sport ________
work ________	short ________	spark ________
warm ________	shark ________	stork ________
word ________	snort ________	

2 Label the pictures using list words.

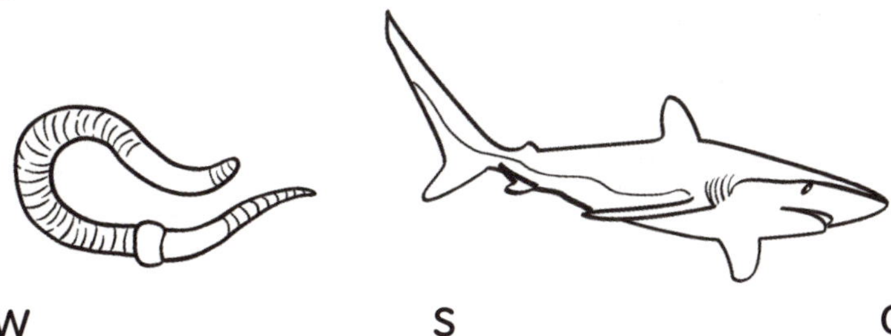

w ________ s ________ a ________ s ________

3 Sort the list words.

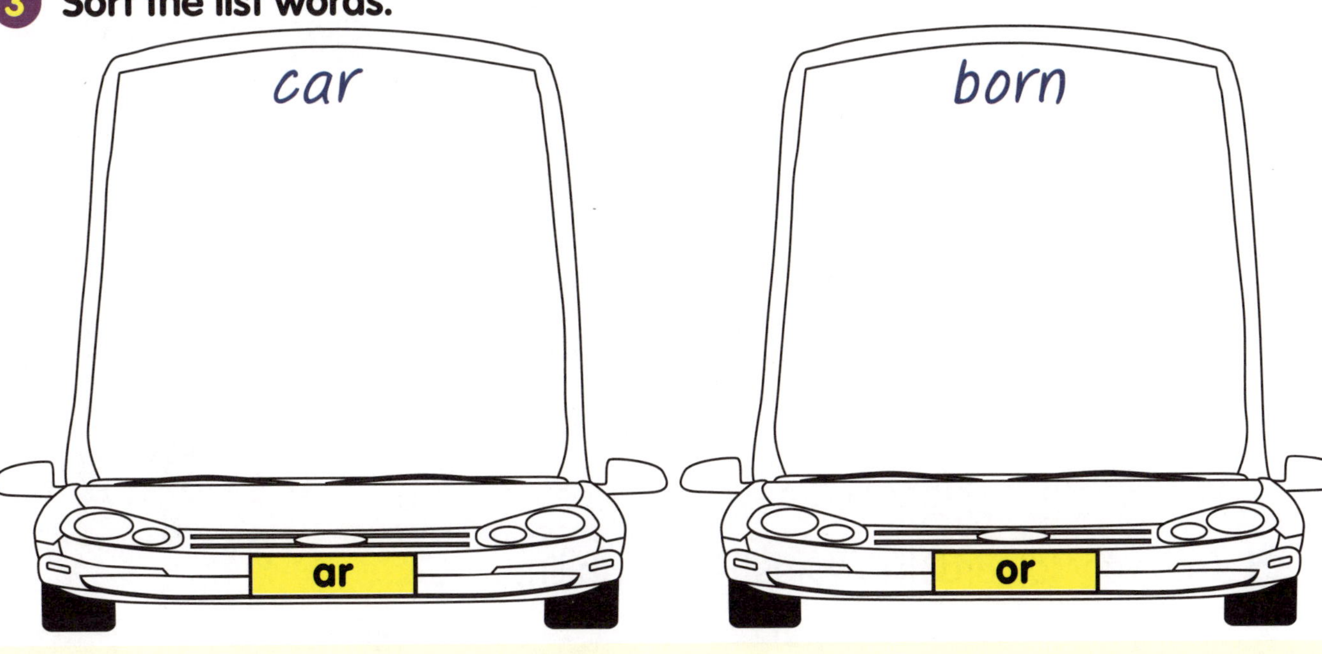

Digraphs: ar, or

1 Complete each sentence with a list word.

a In summer the weather is very ________________.

b Netball is my favourite ________________.

c Mum drove us to school in her new ________________.

d A ________________ has a large fin and lives in the ocean.

e The toad had a huge ________________ on his nose.

Challenge words

2 Copy each challenge word.

morning	__________	worth	__________
corner	__________	wharf	__________
normal	__________	towards	__________
world	__________	worship	__________
worse	__________	remark	__________

3 Make six words using letters from towards.

__________ __________ __________

__________ __________ __________

4 Colour the correct word to complete each sentence.

a I have breakfast in the [morning] [moorning].

b We saw boats dock at the [wherf] [wharf].

c We bought ice cream at the [corner] [cerner] shop.

d They ran [towards] [towords] the finish line.

Collective nouns

A **collective noun** names a **group** of people, animals or things; e.g., a **crowd** of people, a **herd** of cattle.

1 Complete each phrase with a noun from the box.

a a ______________ of sheep

b a ______________ of lions

c a ______________ of shoes

d a ______________ of whales

e a ______________ of bees

f a ______________ of ships

pair	flock
fleet	pride
swarm	pod

2 Draw lines to match the collective nouns to the pictures.

a 

b 

c 

school band litter

3 Write the words next to each phrase under the correct headings.

	Collective noun		Common noun
a	a ______________	of	______________
b	a ______________	of	______________
c	a ______________	of	______________

books	flowers
bunch	gang
thieves	library

Songbird

Making inferences

To make inferences while reading, look for **clues** in the text.

The clues help you find the answers that are hiding in the text.

Read the text.

Circle **who** was in the park.

Box **what** the birds did at the park.

Underline **where** the cages hung.

Colour **what** the grandpas did at the park.

Happy Birds

Lots of cages hung in the trees. Grandpa hung Yan's cage with the others.

There were lots of grandpas and lots of songbirds. All the birds whistled.

The air was full of whistles. Grandpa sat on a bench and whistled too.

Yan liked to sing with the other birds. Grandpa liked to whistle with the other grandpas.

Circle the correct answer.

1. **How** did the birds feel about going to the park?
   - a scared
   - b angry
   - c confused
   - d happy
2. Which **clues** tell you this?
   - a Lots of cages hung in the trees.
   - b Yan liked to sing with the other birds.
   - c All the birds whistled.
   - d Grandpa hung Yan's cage.
3. What **inference** can we make about the birds?
   - a Birds sing when they are happy.
   - b Birds like being in cages at the park.
   - c Birds are good for grandpas.
   - d Birds shouldn't be kept in cages.

Songbird

Read the whole story

Read the letter.

Circle the **colours** of the birds.

Box **how** the birds sing.

Dear Grandpa,

The birds in Australia have bright feathers. Some are grey and pink. Others are white and wear yellow hats. They all sing very loudly.

I wish you could hear the birds, Grandpa. They are happy birds. I am sure Yan would be happy in Australia. You would be happy too.

I miss going to the park with you, Grandpa.

Love, Ling

Underline **what** Ling wants.

Colour **what** Ling misses.

1. **How** do we know Ling likes Australian birds?

____

____

____

2. Does Ling want her Grandpa to come to Australia? How do we know?

____

____

____

Endings: y, ey

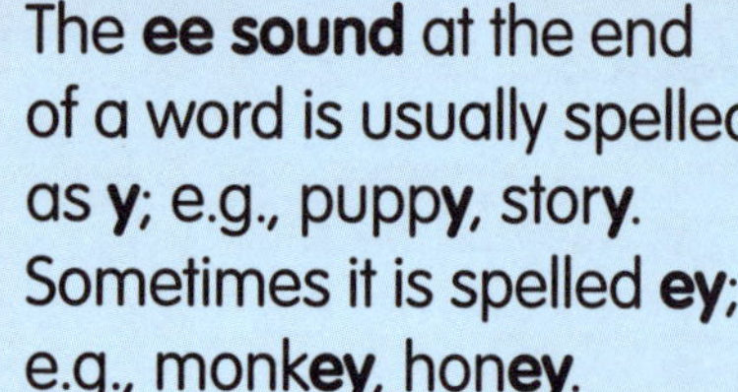

The **ee sound** at the end of a word is usually spelled as **y**; e.g., pupp**y**, stor**y**. Sometimes it is spelled **ey**; e.g., monk**ey**, hon**ey**.

1 Copy each list word.

any ______	worry ______	empty ______
many ______	sixty ______	trolley ______
ugly ______	honey ______	ninety ______
key ______	busy ______	hockey ______
money ______	twenty ______	seventy ______
donkey ______	turkey ______	pretty ______
valley ______	fairy ______	

2 Unscramble the letters to make a list word.

a ckhoey ______ b onmey ______

c nenity ______ d typret ______

e neyho ______ f rutkey ______

3 Write the name for each.

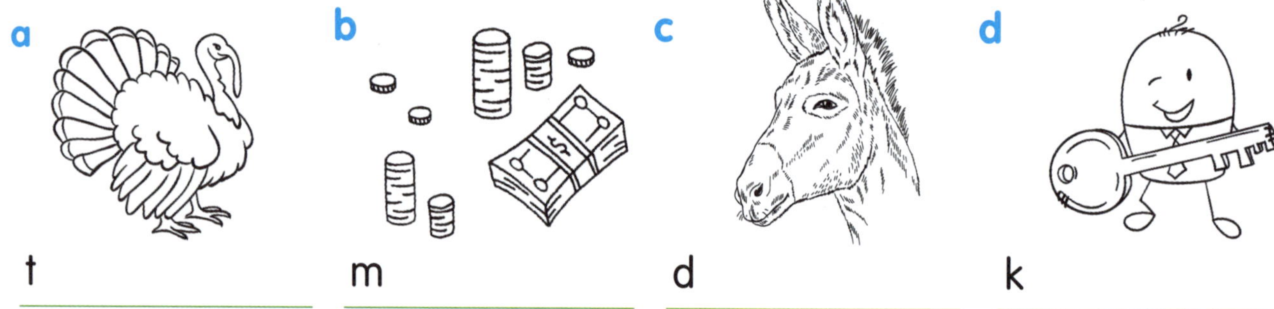

a t ______ b m ______ c d ______ d k ______

4 Underline the spelling mistake. Write the word correctly.

a She put her mony in her purse. ______

b My grandma is ninty years old. ______

c I hope to one day play hocky for the Hockeyroos. ______

Endings: y, ey

1 **Put these list words into alphabetical order.**

fairy any ugly donkey empty

______ ______ ______ ______ ______

Challenge words

2 **Copy each challenge word.**

parsley	______	library	______
family	______	chimney	______
country	______	every	______
jersey	______	January	______
journey	______	February	______

3 **Answer the question with a challenge word.**

a What does smoke come out of? ______

b What is the first month of the year? ______

c Where can you find lots of books? ______

d What grows in your garden? ______

e Who do you live with? ______

4 **Read the clue and complete each sentence using a challenge word.**

a I am a shirt you wear while playing sport. I am a ______.

b I come right after January. I am ______.

c I allow you to read and borrow books. I am a ______.

d I am the land outside big cities. I am the ______.

Week 3 Day 5 Grammar

Proper nouns

A **proper noun** names a particular person, place, animal, thing, day or month. Proper nouns always start with a **capital letter**; e.g., **A**lex, **S**mith, **W**ednesday, **O**ctober.

1 Complete each sentence with a proper noun.

a My name is ______________________________.

b I was born in the month of ______________________________.

c The last month of the year is ______________________________.

d My best friend's name is ______________________________.

e Australia's first female prime minister was ______________________________.

2 Write the names of the days of the week.

______________________________ ______________________________

______________________________ ______________________________

______________________________ ______________________________

____

3 In each sentence, underline the word that needs a capital letter. Write it correctly in the space.

a I let ben ride my bicycle. ______________________

b I decided to call my dog bailey. ______________________

c We are going on holiday in july. ______________________

d Our neighbours' surname is brown. ______________________

e Aunt hilda is coming to visit us. ______________________

Week 4 Day 1 Comprehension

Miss Feline's Unusual Pets

Finding the main idea

The main idea of a text is its key point. It sums up what the text is about.

Details in the text can help you find the main idea.

Read the passage.

Circle the **animals**.

Box Stella's **dialogue**.

Underline **how** the goose came through the window.

Colour **what** made Stella yell.

More Unusual Pets

A goose flew in through the window. She landed with a thump. She grumbled as she got up off the floor.

Then a hyena came to the door. He had the hiccups. He saw the goose and laughed.

They began to argue. It went on and on until Stella yelled, "Stop!"

The room was silent. The crocodile stood very still.

Circle the correct answer.

1. What is the **main idea** of the text?

   a Stella has ordinary pets.
   b Stella doesn't want the animals to fight.
   c Stella is excited.
   d Stella is angry with the goose.

2. Which sentence **supports** the **main idea**?

   a A goose flew in through the window. She landed with a thump.
   b Then a hyena came to the door. He had the hiccups.
   c They began to argue. It went on and on until Stella yelled, "Stop!"
   d The room was silent. The crocodile stood very still.

Miss Feline's Unusual Pets

Read the passage.

Circle the rabbit's **dialogue**.

Box **how** the lion **felt**.

Rabbit Chase

"Help! Help!" yelled the rabbit. "The lion is trying to eat me!"

"I am not," said the lion. He sounded hurt. "I was trying to whisper in your ear. But one of your whiskers tickled my nose. I just slipped."

"Then your foot was in my mouth. I don't know how that happened. Mmmmmm, yummy."

Underline the lion's **dialogue**.

Colour the **clue** that the lion could taste the rabbit.

1. Fill in the missing words.

   The main idea of the text is that the ______________________

   tried to eat the ______________________.

2. Which **two details** helped you find the **main idea**?

   a The rabbit says, ______________________

   ____

   b The lion says, ______________________

   ____

Week 4 Day 3 Spelling

scr, spr, str

In words that start with the letters **scr**, **spr** and **str**, you can hear all three letters in the sound; e.g., **scr**eam, **spr**ang, **str**ung.

1 Copy each list word.

street ______	sprint ______	stream ______
spray ______	scrape ______	string ______
scrub ______	strip ______	scream ______
strong ______	strain ______	streak ______
stroke ______	struck ______	stride ______
strap ______	stripe ______	spring ______
strike ______	screen ______	

2 Sort the list words.

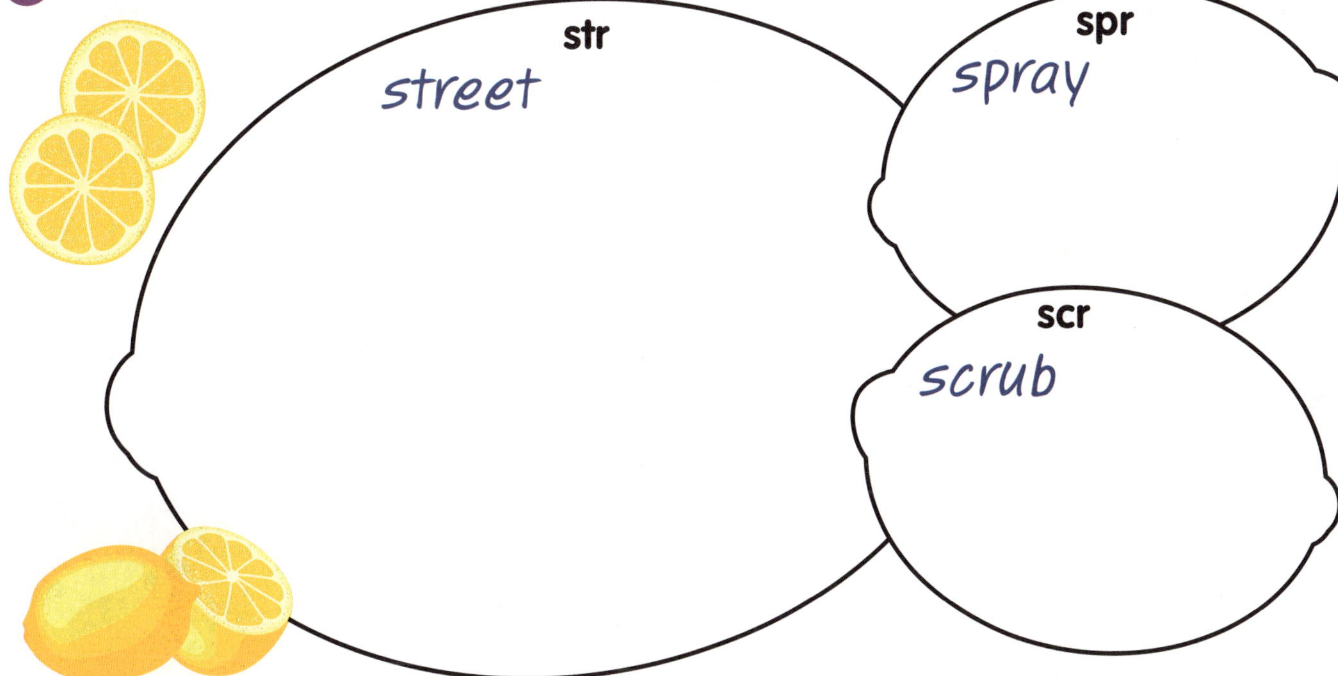

3 Match these list words to their word shapes.

street strap stroke

a

b

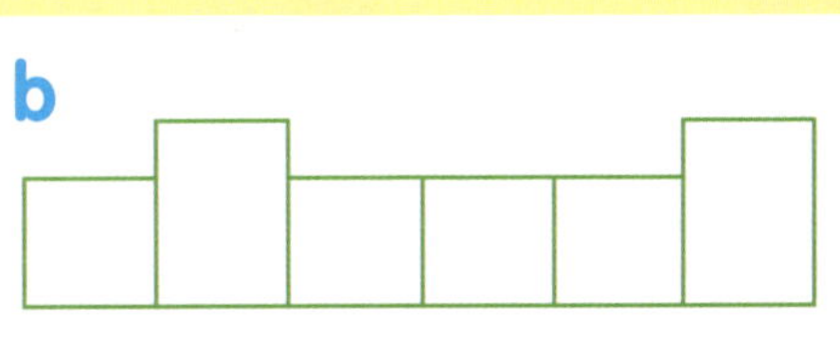

c

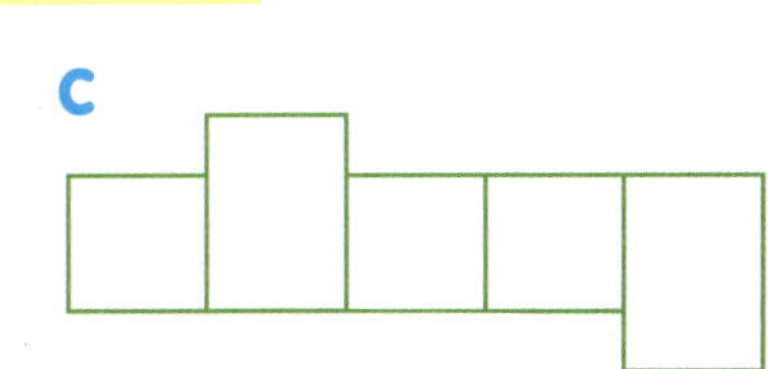

scr, spr, str

1 Underline the spelling mistake. Write it correctly.

a The kitten played with the ball of streng. ______

b I came second in the sprent. ______

c My sister was blocking the television scren. ______

d Our dog has a white strype on his head. ______

e On hot days we swim in the cool streem. ______

Challenge words

2 Copy each challenge word.

strange	______	strength	______
stroll	______	struggle	______
scribble	______	screech	______
scramble	______	strict	______
sprinkle	______	sprout	______

3 Colour the correct word to complete each sentence.

a Our new coach is very [stroll] [strict].

b We took a [stroll] [strange] through the gardens.

c I saw the car [screech] [scribble] to a stop.

d I used my umbrella when it started to [sprinkle] [sprout].

4 Use as many challenge words as possible to make a silly story.

Personal pronouns

A **pronoun** stands in place of a **noun**. Using pronouns saves us repeating nouns all the time; e.g., Jacob said **Jacob** would help **Mia**. Jacob said **he** would help **her**.

1 Circle the pronoun that correctly completes each sentence.

a (Me, I) have a dog and a cat.

b (They, Them) are playing in the garden.

c I gave (he, him) an art set for his birthday.

d Why is (she, her) standing in the rain?

e Grandma and Grandpa are coming to visit (us, we).

2 Complete each sentence with a personal pronoun from the box.

a Riley helped ________________ with my model aeroplane.

b ________________ are eating their lunch.

c Have ________________ made your bed?

d She dropped ________________ on the floor.

e ________________ can't find her saxophone.

me	you	
She	it	They

3 Draw lines to match the pronoun to the picture.

a 

b 

c 

d 

him it them her

Week 5 Day 1 Comprehension

The Ant and the Dove

Finding the main idea

The main idea of a text is its key point. It sums up what the text is about. Details in the text can help you find the main idea.

Read the passage.

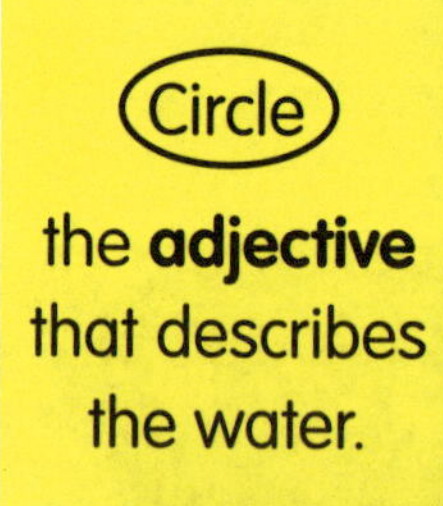

A thirsty ant came to the edge of a river to get a drink. The fast-moving water splashed the ant and knocked it into the river. The ant was in trouble! It tried to swim but it was drowning.

A dove sitting in a tree picked a leaf and dropped it in the river, near the ant. The ant climbed onto the leaf and floated to safety on the bank of the river.

Box **what** the dove did with the leaf.

Circle the correct answer/s.

1. Which **best** describes the main idea of the text?
   - a A dove saved an ant.
   - b An ant fell in the water.
   - c An ant was thirsty.
   - d A dove was flying by the river.

2. Which **two details support** the **main idea**?
   - a The water was moving quickly.
   - b Ants aren't good swimmers.
   - c A dove dropped a leaf in the river.
   - d The leaf floated to safety.

3. Which **best** describes the dove's actions?
   - a excited
   - b kind
   - c worried
   - d angry

The Ant and the Dove

Read the passage.

what the hunter did when he saw the dove.

Box

why the dove flew away.

Underline

what the ant did to the hunter.

A little while later, a hunter came to the edge of the river. He saw the dove sitting in the tree and quickly drew his bow and aimed at the resting bird. The ant saw what was about to happen. It ran over to the hunter and bit his toe as hard as it could. The hunter cried out and dropped his bow. The dove was startled and flew away to safety.

1. Fill in the missing words.

   This text is about how the ______________________

   saved the ______________________.

2. Which **two details** helped you find the **main idea**?

   a The ant ______________________

   ____

   b The hunter ______________________

   ____

Digraph: qu

Two letters that make a single sound are called a **digraph**. The letters **qu** make the **single sound kw**; e.g., **qu**iz, **qu**ote, **qu**ick.

1 Copy each list word.

queen ______	quill ______	quake ______
quiz ______	quilt ______	squint ______
quack ______	quote ______	query ______
quit ______	equal ______	quiver ______
quite ______	equip ______	squeak ______
quest ______	quail ______	squirrel ______
quiet ______	quaint ______	

2 Write a rhyming word from the list.

a shake, make, ______

b scene, bean, ______

c shiver, liver, ______

d wrote, float, ______

e chest, best, ______

f whizz, fizz, ______

3 Which list word answers the riddle?

a I live in a castle and sit on a throne. ______

b A mouse can make this sound. ______

c I like acorns and have a big furry tail. ______

d You put me on your bed when it gets cold. ______

e A duck makes this sound. ______

4 Write the name for each.

a

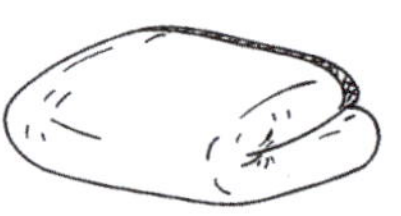

q ______

b

q ______

c

s ______

Digraph: qu

1 Complete the list words.

a __qua__ b ____it c eq__i__

d q__es__ e qu__t__ f qu__i__t

Challenge words

2 Copy each challenge word.

queasy	______	sequin	______
squelch	______	require	______
qualify	______	quench	______
quarrel	______	question	______
frequent	______	squabble	______

3 Colour the correct word to complete each sentence.

a I felt [queasy] [qweasy] after eating too many lollies.

b I drank water to [qwench] [quench] my thirst.

c I raised my hand to ask her a [question] [qwestion].

d I felt the snail [sqwelch] [squelch] under my shoe.

4 Rearrange the chunks to make a list word.

a qu fre ent ______

b ab squ ble ______

c es on ti qu ______

d en ch qu ______

e el ch squ ______

Articles and nouns

Articles are the words **a, an** and **the**. You use them with nouns; e.g., **a** cow, **an** egg, **the** book. Use **a** in front of a word that starts with a consonant sound; e.g., **a** taco. Use **an** in front of a word that starts with a vowel sound; e.g., **an** apple.

1 Fill in *a* or *an*.

a There is ______ fly in my soup.

b The story is about ______ astronaut.

c ______ ant is ______ insect.

d She drew ______ picture of ______ clown.

e He read ______ book about ______ elephant.

2 Complete the story by filling in *a*, *an* or *the*.

Once upon **a** __________ time there was **b** __________ girl called Lily. She went to **c** __________ shops to buy **d** __________ ice cream. On **e** __________ way she met **f** __________ armadillo. She got **g** __________ shock!

3 Complete the labels with *a* or *an*.

a

______ alligator

b

______ zebra

c

______ octopus

Week 6 Day 1 Comprehension

Summer

> **Finding facts and information**
> To find facts and information in a text, ask the questions **Who? What? Where?** or **When?** The answers can be clearly seen in the text.

Read the passage.

what flowers make in summer.

Box

what covers trees in summer.

Plants in Summer

Plants grow quickly in summer.

Many plants flower in summer. Flowers make seeds. Some flowers, like apple blossoms, become fruit. Fruit grows and ripens in the summer.

In summer, trees are covered in green leaves. The leaves make food for the tree. The trunk grows thicker.

Colour

what happens to fruit in summer.

Underline

what happens to tree trunks in summer.

Circle the correct answer.

1 **When** do apple blossoms become fruit?

a summer b spring c winter d autumn

2 **What** do the leaves of a tree do in summer?

a attract insects b make food for the tree
c make roots d protect the trunk

3 **What** ripens in summer?

a leaves b trees c fruit d flowers

Summer

Read the passage.

Underline summer **activities**.

Summer Food

We eat more fresh food in summer.

Salads are made from fresh summer vegetables. Families enjoy the outdoors by having picnics and barbecues.

Many fruits, such as berries, melons and peaches, are ripe in the summer. Fruit salad is good for you and tastes good too.

1. **What** do we eat more of in summer? ____________________

2. **What** ingredients go into a salad? ____________________

3. **Where** do families enjoy barbecues? ____________________

4. **What** are some summer fruits? ____________________

5. **What** can be made with summer fruits? ____________________

Week 6 Day 3 Spelling

Suffixes: ing, ed

Adding the **suffix ing** to a verb shows that something is still happening; e.g., wash**ing**. When the **verb ends in e**, drop the e before adding ing; e.g., ride → rid**ing**.

Adding **ed** to a verb shows that something has already happened; e.g., ask**ed**. When the verb **ends in e**, just add **d**; e.g., hop**ed**.

1 Copy each list word.

saving ______		
closed ______	agreed ______	shaped ______
hiking ______	giving ______	writing ______
freed ______	sharing ______	gazing ______
posing ______	changed ______	solved ______
used ______	phoned ______	exploded ______
raced ______	wasting ______	
chased ______	teased ______	

2 Sort the list words.

ing

saving

ed

closed

3 Unscramble the letters to make a list word.

a sedclo ______ **b** hsaring ______

c kihing ______ **d** singpo ______

e angedch ______ **f** eedfr ______

Suffixes: ing, ed

1 Underline the spelling mistake. Write the word correctly.

a The dog chaased the cat around the garden. ______

b The balloon explooded in her face. ______

c He finally sollved the puzzle. ______

d I agred to help set up the bake sale. ______

Challenge words

2 Copy each challenge word.

arriving	______	created	______
argued	______	freezing	______
chuckling	______	survived	______
caused	______	completed	______
shining	______	compared	______

3 Colour the correct word to complete each sentence.

a The weather was [freezing] [freezeing] outside.

b My brother and I [createed] [created] a secret language.

c We will be [arriveing] [arriving] late because of traffic.

4 Use as many challenge words as possible to make a silly story.

______

______

______

______

Punctuating sentences

A **sentence** starts with a **capital letter** and ends with a **full stop**. If the personal pronoun **I** appears in the sentence, it is written with a **capital letter**; e.g., **M**y brother and **I** set the table**.**

1 Circle the words that need capital letters.

a the Moon is big and bright tonight.

b my friend and i went to the beach.

c the hen has laid some eggs.

d my puppy sleeps in a basket.

e noah and i were riding our scooters.

2 Fill in the capital letters and full stops.

a there is someone at the door

b my sister can play the trumpet

c my brother and i have our own rooms

d our cousins like their new house

e emma and i have finished our chores

3 Write the sentences with the correct punctuation.

a the baby is eating his food

____

b ruby and i are sisters

____

Week 7 Day 1 Comprehension

Dry

Compare and contrast

To compare and contrast information, look for the **similarities** and **differences** between details in the text.

Read the passage.

Box **what** is hard for all animals to find in a dry place.

how large mammals find water.

Underline **how** bilbies and kangaroo rats get water.

Finding Water

Water is hard to find in a dry habitat.

Birds and large mammals, such as antelopes, elephants and zebras, travel long distances to find water.

Other animals get water from the food they eat. Australian bilbies and kangaroo rats get water from insects, fruit, seeds and leaves.

1. Put a [✔] next to information that is true. Put a [✘] next to information that is false.

a ☐ Antelopes and elephants are mammals.

b ☐ It is hard for all animals to find water in a dry habitat.

c ☐ Zebras drink more water than any other animal.

d ☐ Bilbies and kangaroo rats are ocean animals.

e ☐ Fruit, seeds and leaves can give some animals water.

f ☐ Zebras are large mammals.

Dry

Read the full text

Read the passage.

Box **what** special strategies all desert animals have.

Colour **how** kangaroo rats and fennec foxes stay cool.

Conserving Water

Desert animals have special water-saving strategies.

Some animals in dry habitats do not sweat to cool down. This helps the kangaroo rat and the fennec fox to conserve water.

Reptiles have thick skins. Spiders and insects have exoskeletons. These hard, outer shells reduce water loss.

Underline **how** reptiles stay cool.

1 Put a [✔] next to information that is true. Put a [✘] next to information that is false.

a [ ] The fennec fox does not sweat to help it cool down.

b [ ] All desert animals have ways to conserve water.

c [ ] Kangaroo rats have thick skins to help them save water.

d [ ] Spiders have exoskeletons to keep cool.

e [ ] Desert animals need to always be near water.

f [ ] An exoskeleton can help an animal reduce water loss.

Week 7 Day 3 Spelling

Prefix: un

Adding the **prefix un** to a word turns it into its **opposite**; e.g., **un**pack.

1 Copy each list word.

undo ______	unmade ______	unhappy ______
undid ______	unfair ______	undone ______
untie ______	unlike ______	unroll ______
unwise ______	unstuck ______	unable ______
unsafe ______	untrue ______	unwind ______
unfit ______	untidy ______	unload ______
unkind ______	unlock ______	

2 Write the opposites from the list.

stuck unstuck
a happy ______
b roll ______
c able ______
d kind ______
e made ______
f wind ______
g true ______

3 Write the missing letters to complete the list words.

a _ _ fai _
b _ nlik _
c _ _ wis _
d _ _ load
e u _ sa _ e
f _ _ fi _

4 Build a word.

a un + true = ______
b un + fold = ______
c un + happy = ______

Prefix: un

Challenge words

1 **Copy each challenge word.**

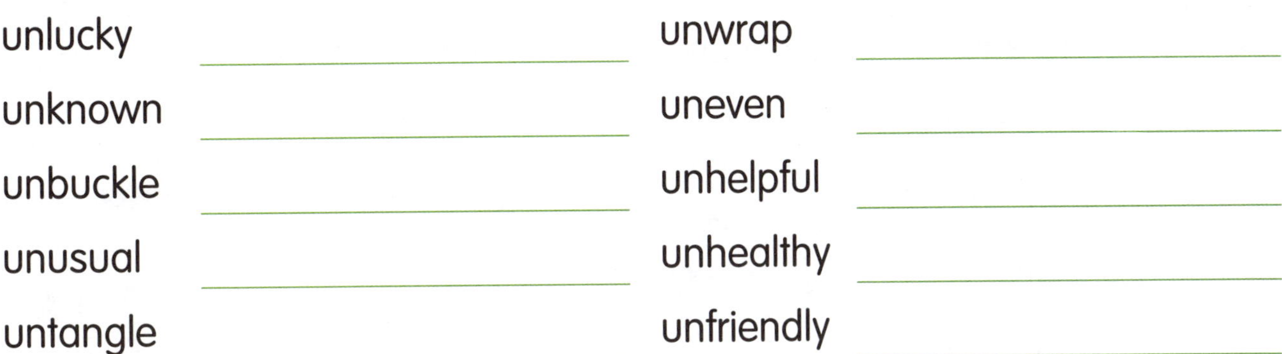

unlucky	______	unwrap	______
unknown	______	uneven	______
unbuckle	______	unhelpful	______
unusual	______	unhealthy	______
untangle	______	unfriendly	______

2 **Make six words using the letters in unfriendly.**

______ ______ ______

______ ______ ______

3 **Colour the correct word to complete each sentence.**

a Some people think that black cats are [unlucky] [unluky].

b I will [unwrappe] [unwrap] my birthday presents.

c The [unfriendly] [unfrendly] dog barks.

d I helped my sister [unbuckel] [unbuckle] her seatbelt.

4 **Find the hidden challenge word.**

a djfunhealthysfdf ______

b dfdunhelpfuldfsdfv ______

c dfdfunusualdfdfs ______

d dfdduntangledfd ______

Adjectives

Adjectives give information about **nouns** and **pronouns**; e.g., **three** kittens, a **disgusting** smell, **happy** children, a **kind** person.

1 **Complete each sentence with an adjective from the box.**

a I like to swim on ________________ days.

b My friend has a ________________ cat.

c There are ______________ eggs in the carton.

d My dad bakes ____________________ pies.

e I was __________________ when I saw the mess.

angry six
furry hot
delicious

2 **Write the adjectives under the correct heading.**

blue twelve brown bitter sweet
twenty purple seven spicy

How many?	What colour?	What taste?
________________	________________	________________
________________	________________	________________
________________	________________	________________

3 **Circle the adjectives that could describe the pizza.**

delicious

crispy

square

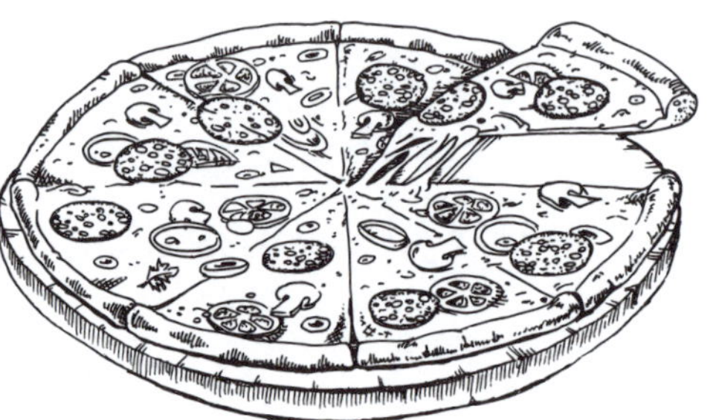

round

lazy

hot

Trains

Finding the main idea

To discover what a text is about, look for the main idea or key point.

Facts and details in the text can help you find the main idea.

Read the passage.

which trains were pulled by steam engines.

Box **how** steam is made.

Underline **what** steam engines burn.

Colour **when** steam trains were used.

Old Trains

The first trains were pulled along by steam engines.

Steam engines burn coal. The burning coal heats water to make steam. The steam makes the wheels turn.

In the 1800s steam trains were a quick and cheap way to travel for fun as well as for work. Today most steam trains are for tourists.

Circle the correct answer/s.

1. What is the **main idea** of the text?
   - a to give facts about why train travel is fun
   - b to describe how steam trains burn coal
   - c to explain how steam trains work and were used
   - d to tell others where to ride steam trains

2. Which two sentences best **support** the **main idea**?
   - a Today most steam trains are for tourists.
   - b The first trains were pulled along by steam engines.
   - c In the 1800s steam trains were a quick and easy way to travel.
   - d The steam makes the wheels turn.

Trains

Read the full text

Read the passage.

Colour **how** modern trains are powered.

Box **where** new trains are used.

New Trains

Today, most trains have diesel or electric engines.

The new engines are quieter and cleaner than coal-powered steam engines. Diesel trains are often used in small towns. Many electric trains run in cities.

Some electric trains can travel very fast. They are called high-speed trains. The bullet trains in Japan can travel three times faster than a car.

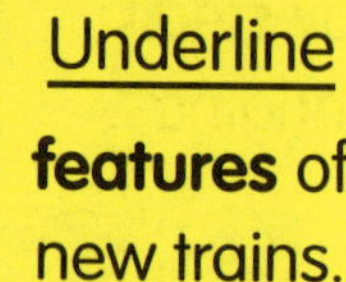

Underline **features** of new trains.

1. Fill in the missing words.

   This text is about different types of ____________________.

2. Give **two details** that support the **main idea**.

   a Most trains ____________________

   ____

   b New train engines ____________________

   ____

Digraph: oo

Two letters that make a single sound are called a **digraph**. The letters **oo** make the **single sound oo**. The digraph oo can make a **long sound**; e.g., f**oo**d, or **short sound**; e.g., c**oo**k.

1 **Copy each list word.**

too	hoot	goose
mood	took	proof
hook	cool	shoot
foot	tooth	loose
wood	broom	groom
room	gloom	ooze
soon	igloo	

2 **Write the name for each.**

a 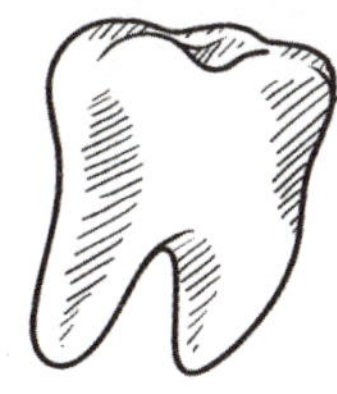

t

b 

i

c 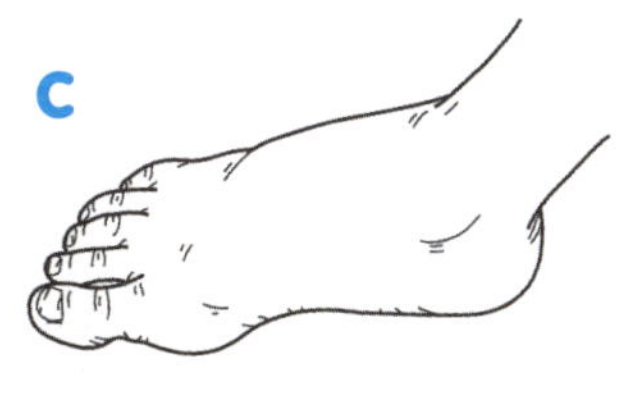

f

d 

h

3 **Sort the list words.**

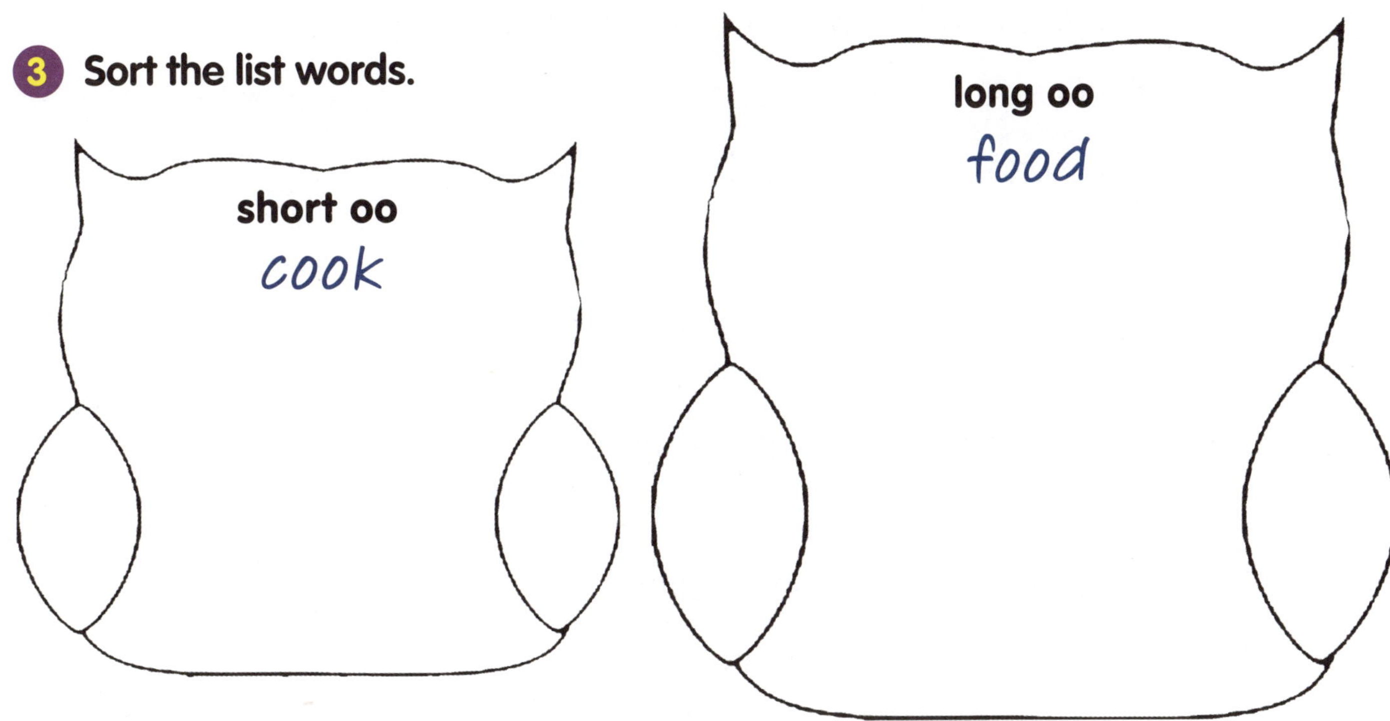

Digraph: oo

1 **Fill in the missing letters.**

a Mum told us to tidy our toy r________.

b I swept up the mess with a b________.

c He cut blocks of ice to build an i________.

Challenge words

2 **Copy each challenge word.**

soothe	________	poodle	________
scooter	________	boomerang	________
rooster	________	kangaroo	________
school	________	snooze	________
goodbye	________	cocoon	________

3 **Read the clue and find the challenge word.**

a I live on a farm and crow very loudly. I am a ________.

b If you throw me, I will come back. I am a ________.

c I have two wheels and a handle bar. I am a ________.

d I am a dog with thick, curly fur. I am a ________.

e A caterpillar goes in, a butterfly comes out. I am a ________.

4 **Answer the question with a challenge word.**

a What do you say when you are leaving? ________

b What do you do if you're feeling tired? ________

c What has a pouch and two large feet? ________

Irregular plurals

A **plural noun** names **more than one** person, place or thing. Most plurals are formed by adding **s** or **es** to the singular; e.g., bird**s**, peach**es**. Some nouns change in other ways when written in the plural; e.g., 1 goose → 2 g**ee**se. Others do not change at all; e.g., 1 sheep → **3 sheep**.

1 Colour the notes with plural nouns.

mice	mouse	women	woman
person	people	ox	oxen

2 Write the underlined word as a plural.

a The dentist filled two of my tooth ________________.

b The child ________________ were making a lot of noise.

c I spotted two wild goose ________________ among the ducks.

d I put on socks because my foot ________________ were cold.

e The woman ________________ are watching the game on TV.

3 Colour THREE nouns that stay the same in the plural.

animal	sheep	moose
cake	deer	horse

Bread

Sequencing events

To identify the sequence of events in a text, look at numbers and words that give clues to the order in which things happen.

Read the passage.

Growing Grain

Wheat, oat, rye and rice are all grains. People eat more grain than any other food.

Farmers grow wheat in large, flat fields. They use machines called cultivators to prepare the soil for planting.

Farmers mix fertiliser with seeds to help the grain grow. They then use a seeder to drop the seeds into furrows.

1. **Order** the events to grow wheat.
   - ☐ Use a seeder to drop seeds.
   - ☐ Mix fertiliser with seeds.
   - ☐ Choose your grain—wheat.
   - ☐ Use a cultivator to prepare the soil for planting.
   - ☐ Choose a large, flat field.

2. What would need to happen **next** for the seeds to grow? Write and draw.

Bread

Read the passage.

Circle **how** the wheat gets to the flour mills.

Box **how long** the grain is soaked.

Underline **what** crushes the wheat.

Refining

Trucks carry wheat to flour mills. The wheat grains are made into flour.

People inspect the wheat to make sure it is good quality.

The grain is cleaned and soaked in water for 10 to 20 hours. This separates the outer layer of bran from the soft, inner part. Rollers crush the wheat into a powder called flour.

1. What happens to the wheat **before** it is soaked?

___

___

2. What happens to the wheat **after** it is soaked?

___

___

3. What does this text explain?

___

___

Week 9 Day 3 **Spelling**

Soft c

The letter **c** makes a **soft s sound** when it comes **before e, i or y**; e.g., pen**ci**l, i**ce**.
Before the vowels a, o, u and some consonants, it makes a **k sound**; e.g., **co**ld, **cr**ack.

1 Copy each list word.

race ________	nice ________	price ________
ice ________	pace ________	space ________
cell ________	trace ________	grace ________
city ________	once ________	spicy ________
mice ________	slice ________	
face ________	twice ________	
icy ________	cycle ________	
lace ________	since ________	

2 Write the name for each.

a r________ **b** f________ **c** c________ **d** m________

3 Fill in the missing letters.

a Her dress was fringed with white l__ __e.

b On my birthday I was given the biggest s__ __ __e of cake.

c I enjoyed the movie so much I saw it t__ __ __e.

d My drink was i__ __ cold.

e O__ __e upon a time there was a princess who was just and fair.

f It was n__ __e of him to stay and help us clean up.

Soft c

1 Match these list words to their word shapes.

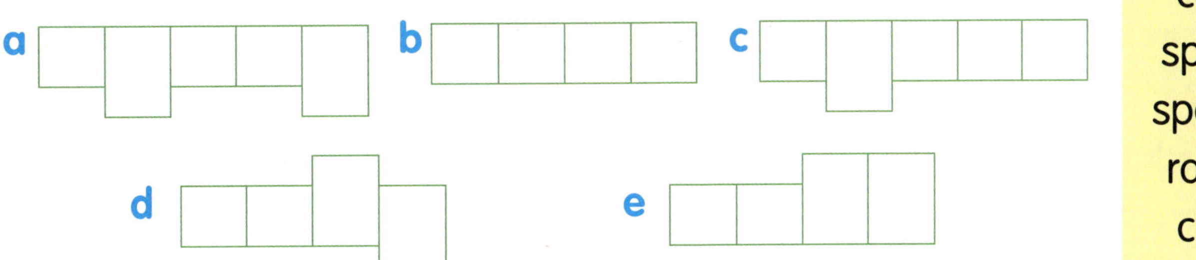

cell
spicy
space
race
city

Challenge words

2 Copy each challenge word.

fleece ______
peace ______
juicy ______
fancy ______
piece ______
prince ______
recite ______
pencil ______
notice ______
excite ______

3 Colour the correct word.

a The peach was so juicy joocy it squirted all over me.
b I used a yellow pencel pencil to colour in the sun.
c The prynce prince was searching for his dragon.
d My boots have a soft flece fleece lining.
e I just wanted one more pece piece of chocolate.

4 Answer the question with a challenge word.

a What comes from a sheep? ______
b What do you write with? ______
c Who is the king's son? ______

Commas in lists

Commas (,) separate words or groups of words in a list; e.g., I have invited **Maya**, **Mark**, **Gina** and **Ben** to my party.

1 Tick [✔] the sentences that have the correct punctuation.

a [ ] My mother bought bread, milk and tomatoes.

b [ ] You can go to the city by train bus, or ferry.

c [ ] Yesterday I played with Jamie, Max, Sam, and Alex.

d [ ] Should I have orange juice, apple juice or pineapple juice?

e [ ] She added the banana peels, eggshells, grass clippings and leaves to the compost heap.

2 Underline the lists.

a I have scratches on my face, feet, knees and arms.

b We saw monkeys, lions, hippos and zebras at the zoo.

c I have drawn a circle, a triangle, a square and a rectangle.

d In my bag are a book, three pencils, a hat and a chocolate.

e The four characters are the king, the queen, the prince and the princess.

3 Use the pictures to help you complete the sentence.

There is a ______________________, a ______________________, a ______________________ and a ______________________ on my bed.

Spelling

Use this review to test your knowledge. It has three parts—**Spelling**, **Grammar** and **Comprehension**. If you're unsure of an answer, go back and read the rules and generalisations in the blue boxes.

You have learned about:

- verb endings: s, es
- scr, spr, str
- prefix: un
- digraphs: ar, or
- digraph: qu
- digraph: oo
- endings: y, ey
- suffixes: ing, ed
- soft c

1 Which correctly completes the word? 1 mark

st __ __ m

a ar b or c ir d er

2 Which word completes the sentence? 1 mark

Charlie __________ carrots in his garden.

a growing b grow c grows d growed

3 Complete each word with *scr, spr* or *str.* 3 marks

a __ __ __ eet b __ __ __ ub c __ __ __ int

4 Correct the word that is wrong in each sentence. 4 marks

a Ali made a spicey curry. __________

b I like to play hocky. __________

c I felt qeasey on the boat. __________

d We were unnhappey with the weather. __________

5 Make four words using the letters from *boomerang.* 1 mark

__________ __________

__________ __________

Your score __ / 10

Grammar

You have learned about:

- common nouns
- personal pronouns
- adjectives
- collective nouns
- nouns and articles
- irregular plurals
- proper nouns
- punctuating sentences
- commas in lists

1 Colour the noun in each circle. 2 marks

a bird sing

b box open

2 Complete each phrase with a collective noun. 2 marks

a a ______________ of cows

b a ______________ of whales

3 In each sentence, circle the word that needs a capital letter. 2 marks

a My best friend's name is amy.

b The first month of the year is january.

4 Replace the noun in brackets with a pronoun. 4 marks

a Annie said (Annie) ______________ didn't have enough money.

b I told Annie I would lend (Annie) ______________ two dollars.

c The children said (the children) ______________ would take the dog for a walk.

d We told the children we would help (the children)

______________.

Grammar

5 Write the correct words. 4 marks

a I added (a, an) __________ egg to (the, an) __________ mixture.

b I put (a, the) __________ cupcakes on (a, an) __________ plate.

6 Complete the sentence with two adjectives. 2 marks

My ______________ friend has ______________ dogs.

7 Write the plurals of the following words. 2 marks

a one foot → two __________

b one man → two __________

8 Fill in the commas. 2 marks

a In one day we had sunshine rain and hail.

b My friend has a dog a cat a guinea pig and a goldfish.

c She added flour sugar butter and eggs to the mixture.

d I have an apple a banana a sandwich and a biscuit in my lunchbox.

Your score

/20

Ringing Guzzler

Read the passage and then use the comprehension skills you have learned to answer the questions.

My dog eats everything. Yesterday he guzzled the sausages in Mum's shopping bag. Last week it was my homework.

This morning Mum couldn't find her mobile phone. She looked on the kitchen bench, in the car, next to the bed. It was nowhere to be seen.

"Okay," said Dad, "I'll use my mobile phone to call your phone."

Guzzler burped. Dad called the number. Yes! There was a faint ring. The sound was coming from somewhere near Guzzler. Oh, no! It was Guzzler! He'd guzzled Mum's phone.

Dad and I laughed, but Mum said, "We'll take Guzzler to the vet to get my phone back, but that's it! I'm going to give him away."

"No, Mum," I cried. "You can't give Guzzler away. He's mine!"

1 Why is the dog called Guzzler? 1 mark — INFERENTIAL

a He likes sausages.

b His owner liked the name.

c He eats everything.

d He has a big belly.

2 What was in Mum's shopping bag? 1 mark — LITERAL

a a mobile phone

b sausages

c a tennis ball

d the writer's homework

Ringing Guzzler

3 Why couldn't Mum find her phone? 1 mark LITERAL

a It was under the bed.
b It was in the car.
c It was in a kitchen drawer.
d It was inside Guzzler.

4 There was a faint ring.
Which word could replace *faint* in this sentence? 1 mark VOCABULARY

a muffled
b clear
c dizzy
d loud

5 How did Mum know where her phone was? 1 mark LITERAL

a She heard it ring.
b She remembered where she'd put it.
c She accidentally tripped over it.
d She saw it on the kitchen bench.

6 What did Dad and the narrator think when they found out what Guzzler had done? They thought it was ... 1 mark INFERENTIAL

a dangerous.
b funny.
c unfair.
d silly.

7 How did Mum feel about Guzzler eating her phone? 1 mark INFERENTIAL

a worried
b confused
c amazed
d angry

8 Who will help Mum get her phone back? 1 mark LITERAL

a the vet
b the doctor
c Dad
d the plumber

9 What does Mum plan to do with Guzzler? 1 mark LITERAL

a sell him
b give him away
c make him stay outside
d lock him up

10 How does the narrator feel about Mum's decision? 1 mark INFERENTIAL

a glad
b disappointed
c upset
d scared

Your score ☐ / 10

Your Review 1 Scores

Spelling		Grammar		Comprehension		Total
☐ / 10	+	☐ / 20	+	☐ / 10	=	☐ / 40

Week 10 Day 1 Comprehension

Take Me to Your Leader

Making inferences

To make inferences while reading, look for **clues** in the text.

The clues help you find the answers that are hiding in the text.

Read the passage.

Circle the **alien's dialogue**.

Box **adjectives** that describe the **alien**.

Underline **how** Tim moves to the wardrobe.

Colour **Tim's dialogue**.

Thump! Thump! Thump!

What is that?

"Thump!"

It's coming from the wardrobe. Tim creeps over and slides the door open. A tiny purple alien steps out and pokes Tim on the foot.

"Take me to your weader!"

Tim jumps back on the bed. The alien is only as big as a teddy bear but he has a zap gun. The gun is pointed at Tim.

"Wha ... what?" Tim asks.

Circle the correct answer.

1. **How** does Tim feel about the alien?

   a scared b angry c confused d happy

2. Which **clue** tells you this?

   a "Thump!"
   b "Take me to your weader!"
   c What is that?
   d Tim jumps back on the bed.

3. What **inference** can we make about Tim?

   a Tim is bigger than the alien.
   b Tim has a very messy room.
   c Teddy bears are Tim's favourite toys.
   d Tim lives on a planet with aliens.

Take Me to Your Leader

Read the whole story

Read the passage.

Colour words that describe **Gweep's appearance**.

Box **Gweep's dialogue**.

Underline **Tim's dialogue**.

Slime Jelly

"Here is some slime instead," Tim yells.

Gweep looks in the bowl. "This bad."

Tim looks at the yummy, wobbly, green jelly. "It's really very nice."

Tears form in Gweep's three round eyes. "It's saying no!"

"The slime isn't saying no. It's shaking because it's scared of you."

"Is it scared?" Gweep smiles. "Of me?"

1. **Why** does Tim pretend the jelly is slime?

2. We can **infer** that Gweep is happy at the end. What is the **clue**?

Week 10 Day 3 Spelling

Plurals with y

Adding the **suffix es** to a **noun** makes it **plural**; e.g., beach**es**.

Adding the **suffix es** to a **verb** makes it **agree with its subject**; e.g., **the bee** buzz**es**.

If the noun or verb **ends in y**, change it to **i** before **adding es**; e.g., injur**y** → injur**ies**, cop**y** → cop**ies**.

1 Copy each list word.

cries ______	babies ______	ladies ______
dries ______	stories ______	entries ______
fries ______	parties ______	worries ______
spies ______	carries ______	replies ______
skies ______	cities ______	studies ______
tries ______	bodies ______	families ______
copies ______	duties ______	

2 Rewrite the word. Change y to i and add es.

a He (try) ______________ to swim.

b She (spy) ______________ on people.

c The (baby) ______________ are crying.

d The (city) ______________ are large.

e He (carry) ______________ the bag.

3 Write the name for each.

a

l ______________

b

b ______________

c

c ______________

Plurals with y

1 Unscramble the list words.

a rrcaies ______________________ b bibaes ______________________

c iesorst ______________________ d iesarpt ______________________

e iesrrwo ______________________ f disesut ______________________

Challenge words

2 Copy each challenge word.

enemies	______________________	injuries	______________________
qualities	______________________	multiplies	______________________
properties	______________________	supplies	______________________
difficulties	______________________	factories	______________________
memories	______________________	libraries	______________________

3 Colour the correct word.

a The soccer players had many [injuries] [injurys] after the game.

b He is having [difficultes] [difficulties] with his computer.

c They are closing down all the old [factories] [factorys].

d If he [multiples] [multiplies] six by two he will get twelve.

4 Write the challenge words in alphabetical order.

______________________ ______________________

______________________ ______________________

______________________ ______________________

______________________ ______________________

______________________ ______________________

Action verbs

Every sentence must have a **verb**. An **action verb** shows what action is happening; e.g., The children **run** in the park.

1 Draw lines to match the action verb to the picture.

a 

b 

c 

d 

e 

eats rides brushes bakes skips

2 Complete each sentence with an action verb from the box.

a I sometimes ________________ dinner.

b She ________________ bread at the bakery.

c They ________________ their bags to the car.

d He ________________ his name on the card.

e Alex ________________ into the pool.

carry	dives	buys
cook	writes	

3 Complete each sentence with an action verb.

a I ________________ the drums.

b I ________________ with a pencil.

c I ________________ at a traffic light.

d I ________________ a ball with a bat.

e I ________________ with a knife and fork.

Mandy Made Me Do It

Visualisation

Good readers imagine pictures when they read a text. This is called visualising.

Looking for key words in the text helps you create images.

Read the passage.

Circle the **noises** Tim made.

Box the **colour** of Tim's nose.

Colour what happened to Tim **after** his star jump.

Underline **how** Mum moved.

Beds Are Not Trampolines

Tim did a star jump. Then he fell off the bed and landed on his nose. He started to cry.

He cried louder and louder. Mum came running into the room and picked him up.

"Now what have you done?" she asked, looking at his red nose.

"Mandy made me do it," Tim sobbed.

Circle the correct answer.

1. Which **key words** tell what Tim did?
   - a running into the room
   - b landed on his nose
2. **How** was Tim feeling?
   - a scared
   - b nervous
   - c excited
   - d sad
3. Which word helps us **hear** how Tim was feeling?
   - a landed
   - b sobbed
   - c nose
   - d fell
4. Which word helps us **see** Tim's nose?
   - a landed
   - b jump
   - c cry
   - d red

Mandy Made Me Do It

Read the passage.

Circle **what** happened to Tim's balloon.

Big Trouble

Tim was in big trouble. He had climbed out the bedroom window to fill a water balloon.

As he turned the water on, his balloon flew off. Water sprayed all over the yard.

Just then, Mum and Aunt Beth stepped into the garden. Both of them were sprayed with water. Boy, were they angry!

Underline **how** Mum and Aunt Beth **felt**.

1. Imagine if you turned on water and it sprayed on you. How would you feel?

____

____

2. Re-read the story. Draw Tim, Mum and Aunt Beth's faces at the end.

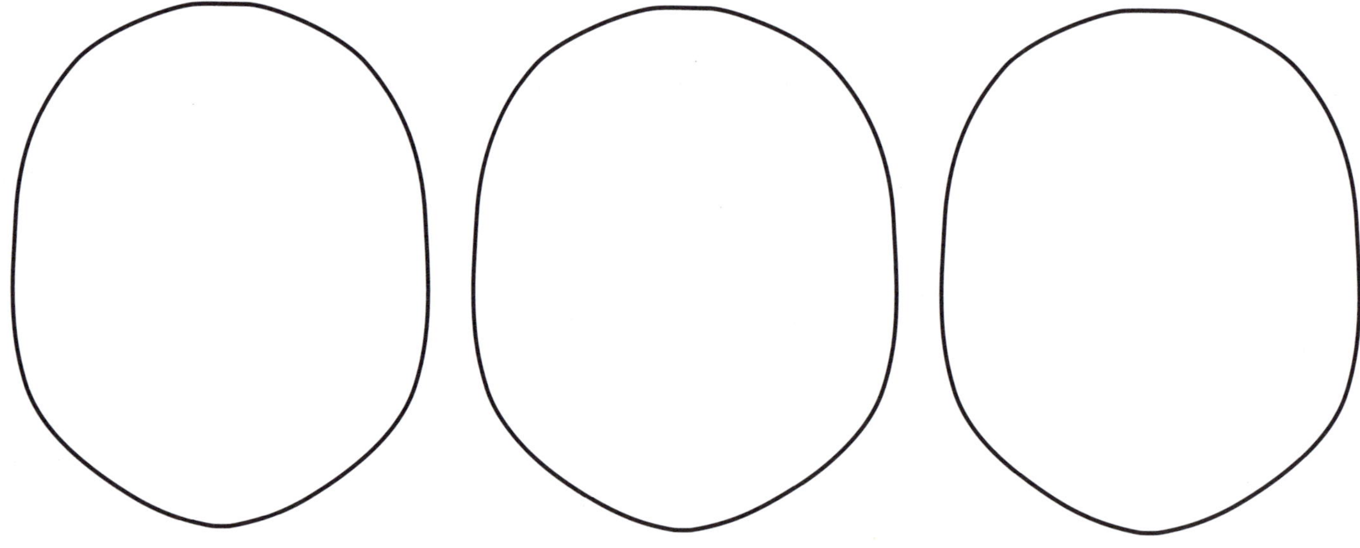

Week 11 Day 3 Spelling

The j sound

The **j sound** is always spelled as **j** **before a**, **o** and **u**; e.g., **ja**r, **jo**b.
The **j sound** is often spelled as **g** **before e**, **i** and **y**; e.g., **ge**m, **gy**m.

1 Copy each list word.

gem ______	germ ______	jewel ______
jar ______	giant ______	adjust ______
jog ______	join ______	Japan ______
jug ______	June ______	magic ______
joke ______	July ______	energy ______
jump ______	angel ______	January ______
jelly ______	giraffe ______	

2 Write the name for each.

a
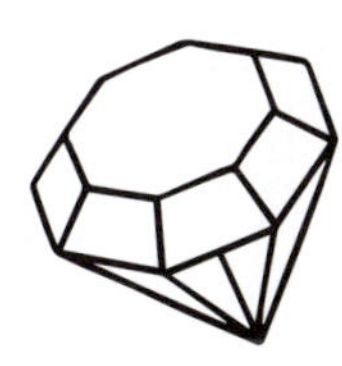
j ______

b

j ______

c

g ______

d

j ______

3 Sort the list words.

The j sound

1 Complete each sentence with a list word.

a We like to _ _ _ _ on the trampoline.

b The _ _ _ _ _ _ _ has a very long neck.

c _ _ _ _ _ _ _ is the first month of the year.

d I poured everyone some juice from the _ _ _ .

e Everyone laughed at Mum's funny _ _ _ _ .

Challenge words

2 Copy each challenge word.

urgent ______	engine ______
agile ______	margin ______
jigsaw ______	juice ______
allergy ______	digit ______
fragile ______	jacket ______

3 Answer the question with a challenge word.

a What do you wear when it's cold? ______

b What is something that you can drink? ______

c What is under the bonnet of a car? ______

d What game has puzzle pieces? ______

e What is another name for a single number? ______

4 Write the challenge words in alphabetical order.

______ ______ ______ ______ ______

______ ______ ______ ______ ______

Present tense

Tense is the form of a verb that shows when an action happens; e.g., The children **play**. (present tense)

1 **Colour the verbs.**

2 **Complete the sentences.**

see is bites go try

My dog Fred and I ____________ to the beach. The beach ____________ near our house. We ____________ a huge crab walking across the sand. I laugh when I see Fred ____________ to play with the crab. The crab ____________ him on the nose.

3 **Underline the word that is wrong. Write it correctly.**

a They talks too much. ____________

b My grandpa live in London. ____________

c We runs to the park. ____________

d Dad drive us to school. ____________

e I likes reading comic books. ____________

Saving Greedy Guts

Finding the main idea

The main idea of a text is its key point. It sums up what the text is about.

Details in the text can help you find the main idea.

Read the passage.

Circle the **verbs** about **eating**.

Gee-Gee?

When I picked him up, Greedy Guts chewed on my fingers. Then he gnawed the strap of my watch.

I put him on the floor and he untied my shoelaces. Then he tried to pull my left sock off. He loved me so much, he wanted to eat me. How could I resist him?

"Mum, please," I begged. "He's perfect."

Underline the **things** Greedy Guts tried to **eat**.

Circle the correct answer/s.

1. Find the **main idea** of the text.
   - a Greedy Guts was bought from a pet shop.
   - b Greedy Guts is perfect.
   - c Greedy Guts likes to eat everything.
   - d Greedy Guts wants to wear socks.
2. Which **two** sentences best **support** the main idea?
   - a "Mum, please," I begged. "He's perfect."
   - b We bought Greedy Guts at a pet shop.
   - c When I picked him up, Greedy Guts chewed on my fingers.
   - d Then he gnawed the strap of my watch.
   - e He loved me so much, he wanted to eat me. How could I resist him?

Saving Greedy Guts

Read the passage.

Circle **who** sent the jacket.

Colour **what** the jacket looked like.

Yesterday was Mum's birthday. Aunt Minnie sent Mum a pink, fluffy jacket. Mum hates pink and she hates fluffy.

"I must ring her to say thank you," Mum said. "Aunt Minnie is a dear to remember my birthday, even if she doesn't remember what I like," Mum said.

"Aunt Minnie is family and you can't choose your family. Mmmm ... perhaps I could wash it and say that it shrank."

Underline **why** Mum got the jacket.

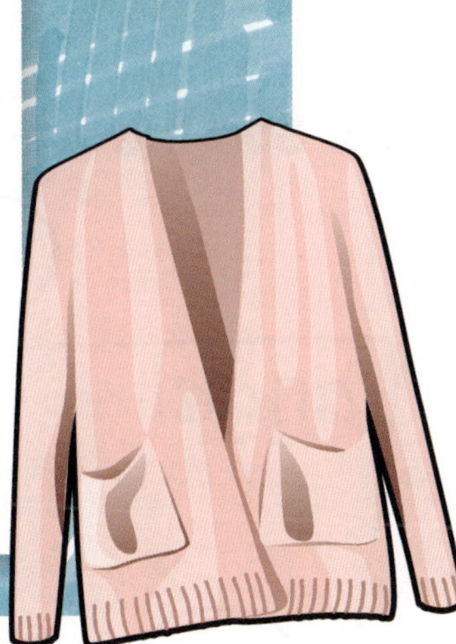

1. Fill in the missing words.

   The text is about what ______________________ thinks of

   ______________________ present.

2. Which **two details** helped you find the main idea?

   a Mum says, ______________________

   ____

   b Mum also says, ______________________

   ____

Week 12 Day 3 Spelling

Endings: le, el, al

Most two-syllable words that end in the **l sound** have the letters **le** at the end; e.g., puddl**e**.

Some two-syllable words that end in the **l sound** have the letters **el** at the end; e.g., cam**el**.

Some two-syllable words that end in the **l sound** have the letters **al** at the end; e.g., flor**al**.

1 Copy each list word.

angel ________	panel ________	title ________
oval ________	level ________	cruel ________
handle ________	camel ________	parcel ________
total ________	tunnel ________	dimple ________
novel ________	puddle ________	towel ________
noodle ________	signal ________	label ________
travel ________	kennel ________	

2 Sort the list words.

el

angel

le

title

al

oval

3 Write the name for each.

a

n ________

b

p ________

c

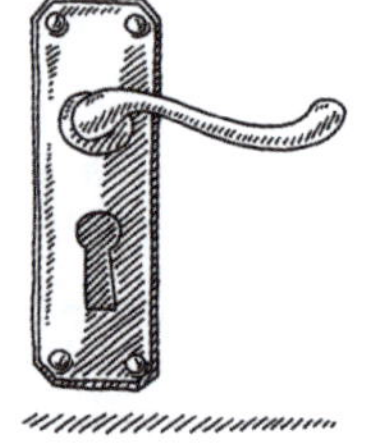

h ________

d

k ________

Endings: le, el, al

1 Underline the spelling mistake. Write it correctly.

a My grandparents sent me a parcal in the mail. ______

b I jumped over the puddel. ______

c I used a towl to dry off after my swim. ______

d You can see her dimpl when she smiles. ______

e We often travl by car on our holidays. ______

Challenge words

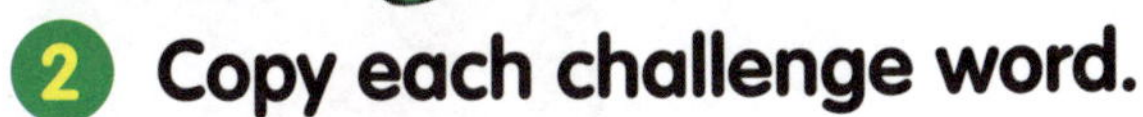

2 Copy each challenge word.

turtle	______	shovel	______
buckle	______	cereal	______
people	______	capital	______
enamel	______	hospital	______
double	______	possible	______

3 Colour the correct word.

a Dad told us all to [buckle] [buckal] our seatbelts.

b I helped [shovle] [shovel] mulch onto the garden.

c We ate [cerele] [cereal] for breakfast.

d Lots of [people] [peopel] live in our town.

4 Word clues. Which challenge word matches?

a twice the amount ______

b a place where sick people are cared for ______

c a reptile with a soft body and hard shell ______

Full stops and question marks

A **sentence** is a group of words that makes complete sense. All sentences start with a capital letter. Sentences that tell something end with a **full stop** (.); e.g., Ollie is reading. Sentences that ask something end with a **question mark** (?); e.g., What is Ollie doing?

1 Fill in the missing punctuation.

a Joseph is writing a story

b What is in the bucket

c When does the show start

d Layla is helping her mother

e Where are my shoes

f The children are playing with their toys

g My friend has a new skateboard

h Which bag is yours

2 Write a sentence that tells what the boy is doing.

____

____

3 Write a question for this picture.

____

____

Week 13 Day 1 **Comprehension**

The Dog and His Reflection

> **Visualisation**
> Good readers imagine pictures when they read a text. This is called visualising.
> Looking for key words in the text helps you create the images.

Read the passage.

words that **describe** the **bone**.

Box
where the dog was going.

A dog had a fresh, meaty bone, which a butcher had thrown to him. He was heading home with his wonderful bone, as fast as he could go.

Underline
who gave the dog the bone.

Circle the correct answer/s.

1. **What** did the butcher throw?
   a a bone   b a biscuit   c a treat   d a ball

2. Which **key word** describes the dog's feelings about the bone?
   a fast   b wonderful   c butcher   d thrown

3. Which two words help us **visualise** the bone?
   a butcher   b meaty   c wonderful   d fresh

4. Which words help us **visualise** the dog's speed?
   a wonderful bone   b meaty bone
   c thrown to him   d as fast as he could go

The Dog and His Reflection

Read the passage.

As the dog crossed a bridge over a pond, he looked down and saw himself reflected in the quiet water. The image was like looking in a mirror.

But the dog thought he saw a real dog carrying another bone—a bone much bigger than his! Without thinking, the dog dropped his bone and leapt at the dog in the pond.

what the **dog saw**.

Underline a word that **describes the water**.

1. **Where** did the dog see himself?

   a in the ocean b in a waterfall c in a pond d in a swimming pool

2. Which words helped you **visualise** the water?

   ____

3. **What** did the dog see?

   a a mirror b a bigger dog c a bigger bone d his reflection

4. **Where** can you see your own reflection?

   ____

5. **What** would the dog's reflection have looked like in the water?

   ____

Week 13 Day 3 Spelling

Digraph: wh

Two letters that make a single sound are called a **digraph**. The letters **wh** make the **single sound w**; e.g., **wh**isper, **wh**ip.

1 Copy each list word.

war ______	whip ______	worm ______
was ______	which ______	whale ______
wipe ______	witch ______	wheat ______
went ______	white ______	wheel ______
when ______	where ______	watch ______
what ______	world ______	while ______
wash ______	wall ______	

2 Underline the spelling mistake. Write the word correctly.

a People once believed the whorld was flat. ______

b She uses shampoo to whash her hair. ______

c The snowy owl has wite feathers. ______

d He dug a whorm out of the dirt. ______

e I couldn't tell wich pencil was mine. ______

3 The letter thief has left his bag behind! Put back the letters he stole.

a wo_ _ _

b wi_ _ _

c wh_ _

d wh_ _ _

e w_ _ _

f wa_ _

g wh_ _ _

h we_ _

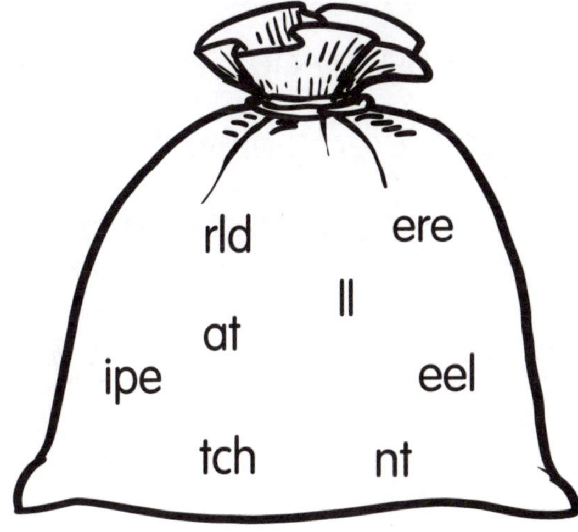

Digraph: wh

1 **Write the name for each.**

a 

w ____________

b 

w ____________

c, d 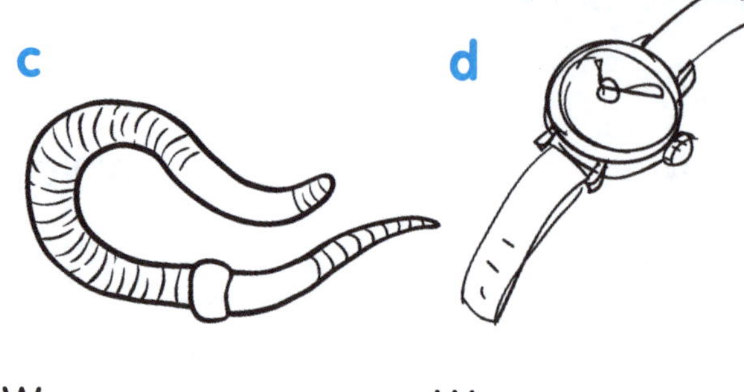

c w ____________

d w ____________

Challenge words

2 **Copy each challenge word.**

whistle	____________	welcome	____________
wagon	____________	whether	____________
whisk	____________	weather	____________
waste	____________	wardrobe	____________
whisker	____________	wheeze	____________

3 **Complete each sentence with a challenge word.**

a She used a _ _ _ _ _ to whip the cream.

b The _ _ _ _ _ was pulled by two strong horses.

c I hung my clothes up in my _ _ _ _ _ _ _ _.

d The referee blew the _ _ _ _ _ _ _ to end the game.

e They have predicted stormy _ _ _ _ _ _ _ all weekend.

4 **Make six words with the letters in wardrobe.**

____________ ____________ ____________

____________ ____________ ____________

Relating verbs

A **relating verb** does not show an action; e.g., I **am** happy. He **is** a tall boy. They **were** excited. We **have** a pet iguana.

1 Circle the correct verb.

a I smile when I (is, am) happy.

b The children (is, are) at the beach.

c I saw them when I (was, were) at the shop.

d The kitten is (be, being) naughty.

e My parents (was, were) very proud of me.

2 Complete each sentence with a verb from the box.

am	is
are	was
were	

a This ______________ a kangaroo.

b Last week my puppy ______________ sick.

c These ______________ elephants.

d I ______________ a drummer.

e Yesterday the kittens ______________ playful.

3 Complete each sentence with a verb from the box.

have	has	had

a A tree ______________ branches and leaves.

b Birds ______________ feathers, beaks and wings.

c Yesterday I ______________ pizza for dinner.

From Farms to You

Sequencing events
To identify the sequence of events in a text, look at numbers and words that give clues to the order in which things happen.

Read the passage.

Circle **two ways** of harvesting berries.

Underline what happens to the berries **before** they are cooked.

Berries to Jam

Berries can be eaten fresh. They can also be cooked with sugar to make jam.

1. Berries grow on small bushes or plants in fields and greenhouses.
2. Some farmers use machines to harvest the ripe berries. Others are picked by hand.
3. The berries are washed, trimmed and cut up or mashed. Then, the berries are cooked with sugar until the mixture is thick.
4. Next, the hot jam is poured into jars and sealed to keep it fresh.

1. What happens to the berries **before** they are harvested?

___

2. What happens to the berries **after** they are washed and mashed?

___

3. Where is the jam poured **after** it is cooked?

___

4. What **text feature** tells you the steps must be done in order?

___

From Farms to You

Read the passage.

Cows to Milk

First, the cows are taken to the milking shed.

__________, they are milked using milking machines.

__________, milk tankers take the milk to a factory where it is heated to kill any harmful bacteria.

__________, the milk is put into bottles or cartons and kept refrigerated.

__________, it is taken to shops and supermarkets.

Finally
Then
Next
After this

1. Add the **time adverbs** to complete the passage.
2. Draw **the process** from cows in the milking shed to milk in the supermarket.

Step 1	Step 2	Step 3
Step 6	Step 5	Step 4

Exceptions

Some words are tricky to spell because they contain letters that do not make their usual sounds; e.g., sure, again.

1 Copy each list word.

door	______	past	______	father	______
poor	______	child	______	pretty	______
after	______	hold	______	half	______
even	______	sure	______	hour	______
who	______	sugar	______	grass	______
again	______	prove	______	climb	______
bath	______	great	______		

2 Complete each sentence with a list word.

a I closed my bedroom d_ _ _ .

b He felt p_ _ _ after spending all his money.

c We watch television a_ _ _ _ dinner.

d Six and eight are e_ _ _ numbers.

e I h_ _ _ Mum's hand when crossing the road.

3 Which list word matches?

a			g			makes food and drinks sweet
b			u			60 minutes
c		a				one of two equal parts
d					d	a young person

Exceptions

1 Write the list words from page 74 in alphabetical order.

Challenge words

2 Copy each challenge word.

because	would
behind	should
steak	whole
beautiful	improve
clothes	everybody

3 Underline the spelling mistake. Write the word correctly.

a Dad grilled the stek and vegetables.

b He thought her painting was butiful.

c She ate a wole fruit bar.

d He wished everibody would just get along.

e We went shopping for new cloes.

4 Use as many challenge words as possible to make a silly sentence.

Past tense

The **tense** of a verb shows **when** an action happens; e.g.,
The dogs **walk**. (Present tense → happens now.)
The dogs **walked**. (Past tense → has already happened.)

1 Sort the verbs.

walked push stopped blamed sail fill picked play

Present tense	Past tense
______	______
______	______
______	______
______	______

2 Underline the word that is wrong. Write it correctly.

a Last week Jake fix his bicycle. ______

b I enter the competition last year. ______

c I finish reading the book an hour ago. ______

d Yesterday Hayley visit her grandma. ______

e Last night I watch my favourite show. ______

3 Write these sentences in the past tense.

a I lock the door to the garage.

Yesterday ______

______

______

b I wash the dishes after dinner.

Last night ______

______

______

Week 15 Day 1 Comprehension

Tools

Compare and contrast
This table compares and contrasts everyday tools people use. Look for **similarities** and **differences**.

Read the table.

Tool	Function	Powered by humans	Powered by electricity	Powered by battery
hammer	used to hammer nails, break rocks and remove nails	✓	✗	✗
pen	used to write	✓	✗	✗
blender	used to mix foods and liquids	✗	✓	✗
calculator	used to do maths	✗	✓	✓

1 Put a [✓] next to information that is true. Put a [✗] next to information that is false.

a ☐ Hammers and calculators are both powered by electricity.

b ☐ You must have a battery to use a pen.

c ☐ Batteries power calculators.

d ☐ Pens and hammers are powered by humans.

e ☐ A hammer and a pen have the same function.

f ☐ Blenders are powered by electricity.

Find the answer in the table.

2 Which tools are powered by humans? ____________________

3 Which tools are *not* powered by electricity? ____________________

4 Which tool is powered by battery? ____________________

5 Which tools are powered by electricity? ____________________

Tools

Read the passage.

Colour tools schools used **from** the 1970s.

Box tools schools used **before** the 1970s.

1970s

Many new tools and gadgets became popular in the 1970s.

Prior to the 1970s, most schools used books, blackboards and paper as educational tools.

By the 1970s, many schools had film projectors, record players and tape recorders to help children learn.

By the late 1970s, people began to buy personal computers for their homes.

1 Complete the table using [✔] and [✘].

School Tool	Used before 1970	Used in the 1970s	Used today
Books			
Blackboards			
Paper and pencils			
Film projectors			
Record players			
Tape recorders			

2 Which tools were used **before 1970**?

____

3 Which tools were used before the 1970s and are **still used** in schools today?

____

Week 15 **Day 3** **Spelling**

Plurals: s, ves

A **plural** is more than one. For most nouns that **end in f or fe**, make them plural by **changing f to v** and **adding es**; e.g., leaf → leaves.
Some nouns that **end in f or fe** just need an **s** to become plural; e.g., reefs.
For nouns that **end in ve**, just add **s** to make them plural; e.g., detectives.

1 Copy each list word.

lives ________	elves ________	loaves ________
puffs ________	waves ________	gloves ________
safes ________	stoves ________	giraffes ________
wives ________	leaves ________	cafes ________
reefs ________	sleeves ________	scarves ________
cliffs ________	olives ________	shelves ________
hives ________	wolves ________	

2 Write the singular and plural for each word.

a		________	________	
b		________	________	
c		________	________	
d		________	________	

3 Write the word as a plural.

a I wear (glove) ________ to keep my hands warm.

b We saw lots of (giraffe) ________ at the zoo.

c There are three (shelf) ________ in the wardrobe.

Plurals: s, ves

1 **Sort the list words from page 79.**

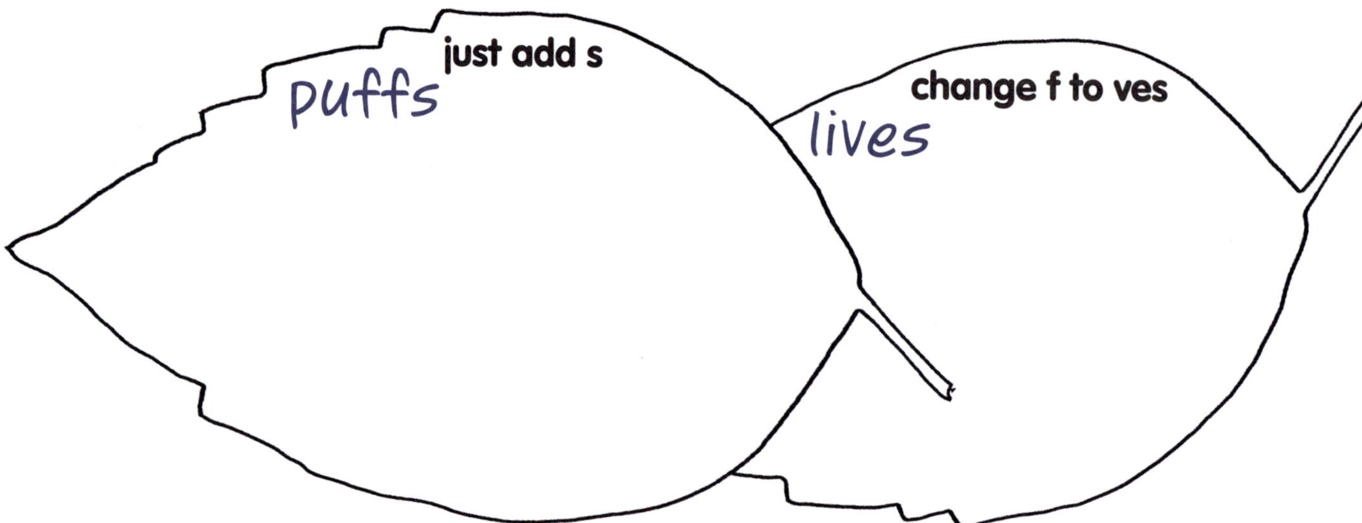

Challenge words

2 **Copy each challenge word.**

knives ______	calves ______
halves ______	grooves ______
sheaves ______	selves ______
thieves ______	flagstaffs ______
nerves ______	detectives ______

3 **Complete each sentence with a challenge word.**

a In the cutlery drawer we have spoons, forks and ______.

b We saw lots of ______ with their mothers on the farm.

c My shoes have ______ on the bottom.

d I cut the orange into two ______.

4 **Use challenge words to make a very silly sentence.**

______

______

Helping verbs

Helping verbs help **other verbs** do their work; e.g., I **am reading**. She **is drawing**. We **are singing**.

1 **Complete each sentence with a helping verb from the box.**

has	have	am	is	are

a The dog ______________ barking at the cat.

b I ______________ making a card for my friend.

c Bella ______________ found her other sock.

d The people ______________ sitting in their seats.

e The children ______________ finished their chores.

2 **Complete the answers to the questions.**

a What is Caleb doing?

Caleb is ____

____

b What are the birds doing?

The birds are ____

____

3 **Underline the word that is wrong. Write it correctly.**

a Michael have baked some cookies. ______________

b The children is swimming in the lake. ______________

c Lily and Phil was singing a song. ______________

Transport

Compare and contrast
Look for **similarities** and **differences** between details in the text.

Read the passage.

Underline the **purpose** of transport.

Box types of **public transport**.

Colour a **word** that means the same as **transport**.

Circle types of **private transport**.

Transport

Vehicles, such as cars, buses, trains, planes and boats, transport us from one place to another.

Some people use transport to make short, daily trips to work or school. Others use it for longer journeys, such as a holiday or business trip overseas.

Public transport is designed for moving large groups of people. Buses, trains, trams, ferries and planes are types of public transport. Private transport includes cars, motorcycles and bicycles.

1 Complete the table about transport.

	Purpose	Examples
Private transport		
Public transport		

2 What does all transport do? ______________________________

Transport

Read the full text

Transport

Read the passage.

Box **when** people began buying cars.

Underline **when** more roads appeared.

Colour **why** Ford's cars were affordable.

Circle **how** road safety became an issue.

Cars

In the early 1900s, people began to buy their own cars. In 1908, Henry Ford began making cars on an assembly line. His factory made cars at a much faster rate. These mass-produced cars were cheaper to buy.

In the 1950s, many more people owned cars. More cars meant more roads. With more cars on the road, people started to think about car safety. The first seat belts strapped across the driver's lap.

1 Make a timeline about cars.

Early 1900s	1908	1950s

2 **When** were cars first mass produced?

a 1901–1910 b 1961–1970 c 1911–1920 d 1951–1960

3 **When** were more roads built?

a 1931–1940 b 1901–1910 c 1951–1960 d 1941–1950

Week 16 Day 3 Spelling

Long oo exceptions

Two letters that make a single sound are called a **digraph**. Many vowel combinations make an **oo sound**. The letters **ou, ui, oe, ue** and **ew** all sometimes make an **oo sound**; e.g., s**ou**p, s**ui**t, can**oe**, bl**ue**, bl**ew**.

Sometimes **the single vowel u** makes an **oo sound**; e.g., fl**u**.

1 Copy each list word.

you		rude		threw	
fruit		grew		blew	
shoe		clue		chew	
blue		crew		screw	
flew		suit		prune	
soup		group		ruby	
true		truth			

2 Name.

a s

b f

c s

d s

3 Match the clue to a list word.

a		u				a deep red gem
b			o			something worn on your foot
c	f					grown on plants
d		r			e	a dried plum
e			u			the colour of the sky

Long oo exceptions

1 Write the missing letters to complete the list words.

a sc__ __ __ b cl__ __ c gr__ __

d cr__ __ e bl__ __ f fl__ __

g ch__ __ h th__ __ __ i s__ __p

Challenge words

2 Copy each challenge word.

bruise	________	should	________
bluish	________	through	________
cruise	________	canoe	________
would	________	cashew	________
could	________	gruesome	________

3 Colour the correct word.

a I [could] [cowld] not stop listening to her new song.

b I screamed as my brother capsized our [canoo] [canoe].

c The movie was too [groosome] [gruesome] to watch.

d The train sped [throo] [through] the tunnel.

4 Complete each sentence with a challenge word.

a I had a large ________ on my leg after falling over.

b I had a packet of ________ nuts for my morning snack.

c I wish that I ________ fly like a bird.

d Mum told me that I ________ go and clean my room.

Future tense

Future tense verbs show that an action will happen in the future. The future tense is formed by writing the helping verb **will** in front of the main verb; e.g., Declan **will** make his bed later. You can also write the words **am going to**, **is going to** or **are going to** in front of the verb; e.g., They **are going to** rest this afternoon.

1 Use the pictures to answer the questions.

a Where will you climb?

I will climb ______________________________

b How are you going to travel?

I am going to travel ______________________________

c When will they arrive?

They will arrive ______________________________

2 Complete each sentence.

a You ______________ miss your train if you don't hurry.

b My father ___________ going to fetch me later.

c I ___________ going to meet them at the park.

d Alex is ______________ to invite me to his party.

e The dentist is going ___________ clean my teeth.

3 Write each sentence in the future tense.

a Yesterday I bought a new model plane.

Tomorrow ____

b Last week I visited my cousins in Queensland.

Next week ____

Postcards

Making connections

Good readers know how to make connections in a text. They link words, ideas and events to themselves, things they have read and real world events.

Read the postcard.

Underline **when** they went to the zoo.

Box **what** they saw at the zoo.

Colour **who** went to the zoo.

Circle **what** they ate at the zoo.

Dear Mum,

Today we got up really early and went to the zoo. It was huge! The giraffes had lots of room and the lions hid in the bushes. Dad pretended to be a mountain goat. We bought ice creams after lunch. Boo-boo had chocolate and I had vanilla. Dad carried us when we got really tired. See you tomorrow!

Love, T

xx

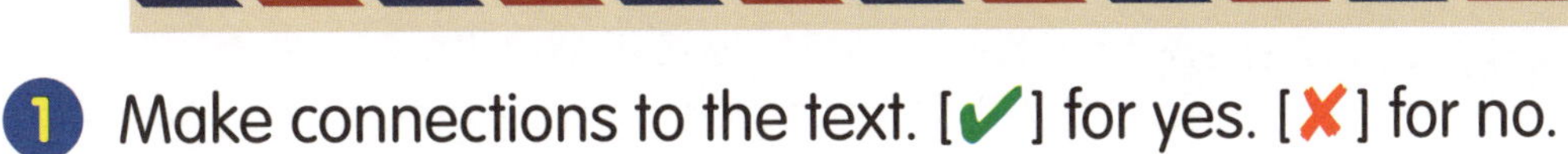

1. Make connections to the text. [✔] for yes. [✘] for no.

   a [ ] Have you ever got up really early?

   b [ ] Have you ever been to the zoo?

   c [ ] Have you ever seen a mountain goat?

   d [ ] Have you ever had ice cream after lunch?

2. Write about one of your connections to the text.

Postcards

Read the postcard.

Underline **when** they arrived in Paris.

Box **what** they thought of Paris.

Dear Anna and Janek,

We arrived in Paris yesterday afternoon. Last night we went up to the top of the Eiffel Tower. The city was all lit up and so pretty. Today we went to three art galleries so I have sore feet! What have you been doing?

Love, Vicky and Sean

Colour **who** is in Paris.

Circle **where** they went in Paris.

Use your knowledge to answer questions about postcards.

1. **What** is a postcard? ____________________
2. **Why** do people write postcards? ____________________
____
3. **What** information do people give in a postcard? ____________________
____
4. Imagine your favourite place to visit. Write two sentences about your adventures there.
____
____
____

Suffixes: ful, less

Adding the **suffix ful** to a noun or verb turns it into an adjective; e.g., pain**ful**, or another noun; e.g., mouth**ful**.

Adding the **suffix less** to a noun or verb turns it into an adjective; e.g., help**less**.

1 Copy each list word.

awful ______	handful ______	grateful ______
useless ______	joyful ______	powerful ______
helpful ______	playful ______	spiteful ______
careless ______	mouthful ______	cheerful ______
spoonful ______	graceful ______	truthful ______
plateful ______	thankful ______	harmless ______
restless ______	forgetful ______	

2 Sort the list words.

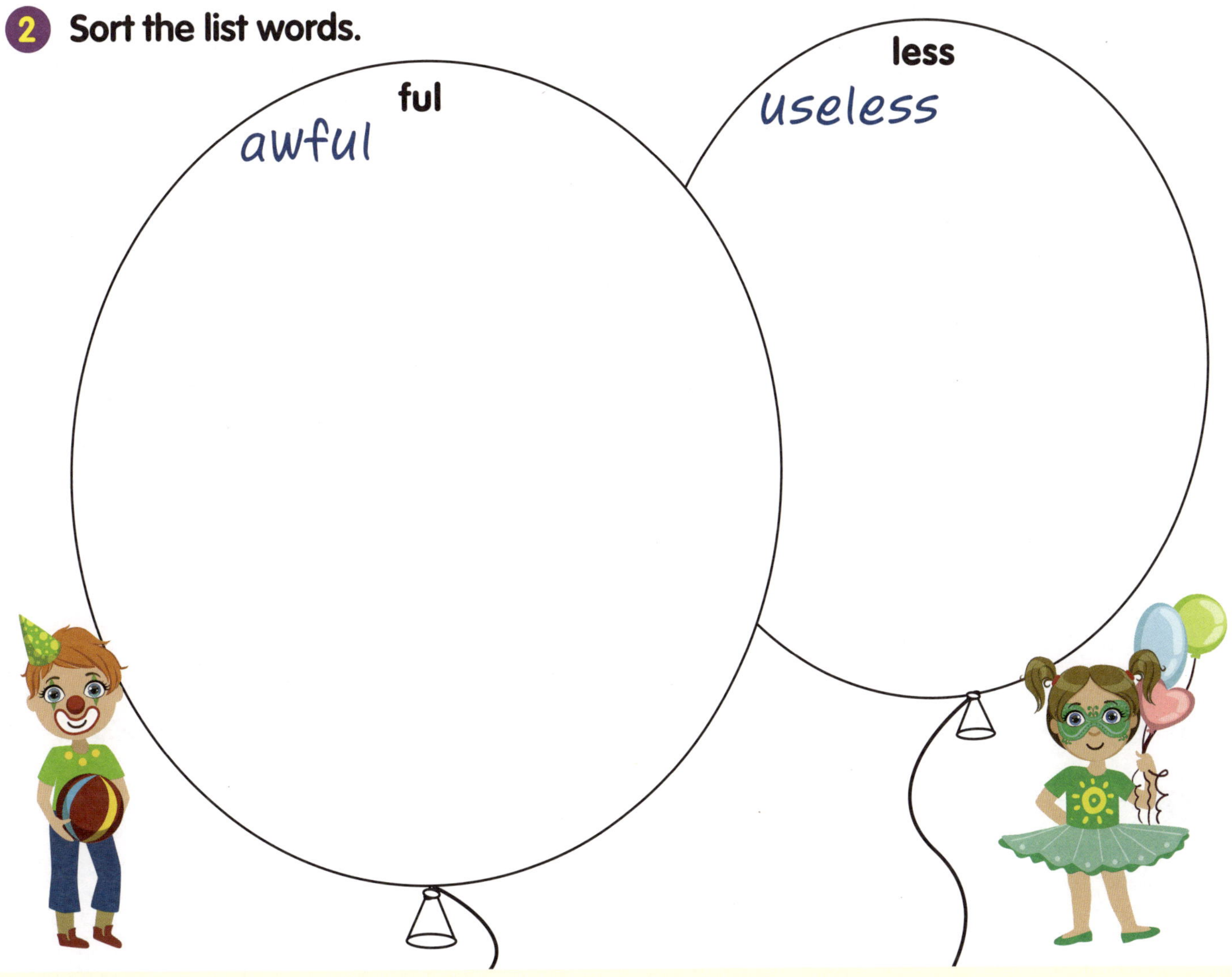

Suffixes: ful, less

1 Underline the spelling mistake. Write it correctly.

a She would only eat a spoonfull of the soup. ______

b Mum gave us each a platefull of pasta. ______

c His careles mistake got him into trouble. ______

d Dad told us he wanted a truthfull answer. ______

Challenge words

2 Copy each challenge word.

beautiful ______

wonderful ______

colourless ______

delightful ______

faithful ______

merciful ______

plentiful ______

houseful ______

peaceful ______

disgraceful ______

3 Complete each sentence.

a We had a p______ supply of food.

b Water is a c______ liquid.

c The coach said I had made w______ progress this season.

d We were punished for our d______ behaviour.

4 Use as many challenge words as possible to make a silly sentence.

______

______

______

Verb groups

Verbs can tell about the action in a sentence. **Adverbs** can give information about action **verbs**. **Adverbs** can tell us more about how an action happens.

1 Underline the verb in each sentence.

a The knight fought ____________________.

b The sun is shining ____________________.

c We divided the pie ____________________.

d The toddler yawned ____________________.

e The hungry animals ate ____________________.

f I wrote my story ____________________ into my book.

g She held ____________________ onto her friend's hand.

2 Complete each sentence in Question 1 with an adverb from the box.

brightly tightly sleepily equally
bravely neatly greedily

3 In the following sentences, complete each answer with an adverb.

a How did he greet his teacher?

He greeted his teacher ____________________.

b How did she answer the questions?

She answered the questions ____________________.

c How did he shout at the children?

He shouted ____________________ at the children.

d How did she run to the classroom?

She ran ____________________ to the classroom.

Signs

Word study

Good readers use clues in the text and their own knowledge to work out word meanings. It helps to understand the author's intention.

Read the signs.

Circle the **compound words**.

Underline the **verbs**.

Box the **title**.

Highlight new **vocabulary**.

KEEP THE WILD IN WILDLIFE

DO NOT FEED THE WATERFOWL

Sign 1

FIRE DANGER TODAY

LOW

MODERATE

HIGH

VERY HIGH

EXTREME

Sign 2

Sign 1

1 Complete these definitions.

Sign 2

2 Complete these sentences.

a The highest fire danger warning is ______________________.

b Extreme means ______________________.

c People feel safest when the fire danger is ______________________.

Signs

Read the sign.

1. **What** does fragile mean? ______

2. Which **clues** helped you to know this? ______

3. **What** do the pictures tell you? ______

4. **Name** three things that are fragile. ______

5. **Where** would you expect to see this sign? ______

Silent letters

Some words have a **silent letter** at the beginning. We say the **second letter**.

Words that are spelled with **kn** or **gn** at the start, begin with the sound **n**; e.g., **kn**ee, **gn**ome.

Words that start with **wr**, begin with the sound **r**; e.g., **wr**inkle.

1 Copy each list word.

know ______

gnat ______

knee ______

wrap ______

knit ______

knob ______

knew ______

wreck ______

write ______

knot ______

knife ______

knock ______

kneel ______

knelt ______

knack ______

gnome ______

wrong ______

wrote ______

wrist ______

gnash ______

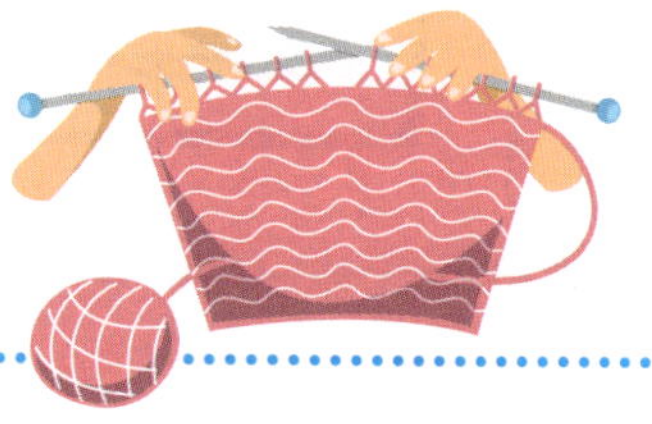

2 Name.

a 

gn ______

b 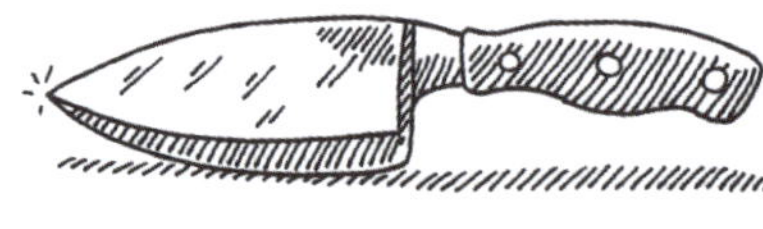

kn ______

c

kn ______

d 

wr ______

3 Fit words into the blocks.

a [ ] [r] [ ] [t] [ ]

b [k] [ ] [ ] [ ] [l]

c [g] [ ] [ ] [s] [ ]

Silent letters

1 Complete each sentence with a list word.

a I heard a ________ at the front door.

b I ________ down to tie my shoelaces.

c My big brother had trouble brushing the ________ out of his hair.

d I hooked the bracelet around my ________.

Challenge words

2 Copy each challenge word.

written	________	wrestle	________
wreckage	________	knight	________
knuckle	________	known	________
wrinkle	________	gnaw	________
wriggle	________	knead	________

3 Complete each sentence with a challenge word.

a I could not get the ring over my ________.

b I watched the worm ________ in the dirt.

c The brave ________ rode away on his horse.

d The ________ from the storm took weeks to clean up.

e The baker must ________ the dough before putting it in the oven.

4 Use as many challenge words as possible to make a silly story.

____

____

____

Full stops and exclamation marks

Sentences that tell something end with a full stop. Sentences that express a **strong feeling**—like fear, surprise or excitement—sometimes end with an exclamation mark (!); e.g., You scared me! Sometimes sentences that express strong feelings can start with **What** or **How** and end with an exclamation mark; e.g., **What** an amazing day that was! **How** good was that!

1 Fill in the missing full stops and exclamation marks.

a Please take a ball and a bat

b What a good child he is

c How exciting was that exhibit

d I gave Ben one of my trading cards

e I've invited Eva and Claire to my party

f I can't wait to ride my new bike

2 Change these sentences to exclamations. Start each sentence with How.

That is very good. *How good is that!*

a That was brilliant. ____________________

b This is exciting. ____________________

3 Change these sentences to exclamations. Start each sentence with What.

That was a great story. *What a great story that was!*

a That is a cute puppy.

____

b That was an exciting ride.

____

Spelling

Use this review to test your knowledge. It has three parts—**Spelling, Grammar** and **Comprehension**. If you're unsure of an answer, go back and read the rules and generalisations in the blue boxes.

You have learned about:

- plurals with y
- digraph: wh
- long oo exceptions
- j sound
- exceptions
- suffixes: ful, less
- endings: le, el, al
- plurals: s, ves
- silent letters

1 Complete each word with *le, el* or *al*. 3 marks

a tow__ __ b ov__ __ c pudd__ __

2 Which word completes the sentence? 1 mark

Eli put a __________ of mashed potato on his plate.

a spoons b spoonless c spoonful d spooned

3 Complete each word with *wh, kn, gn* or *wr*. 4 marks

a __ __ob b __ __ist c __ __ale d __ __ash

4 Which word completes the sentence? 1 mark

I want to __________ Mount Kosciuszko in New South Wales.

a climb b climbed c climbing d climbs

5 Complete. 1 mark

a one party, two __________

b one ruby, two __________

c one scarf, two __________

d one café, two __________

Your score
___
10

Grammar

You have learned about:

- action verbs
- relating verbs
- future tense
- present tense
- helping verbs
- past tense
- full stops and question marks
- verb groups
- full stops and exclamation marks

1 Colour the action verb in each circle. 2 marks

a

b
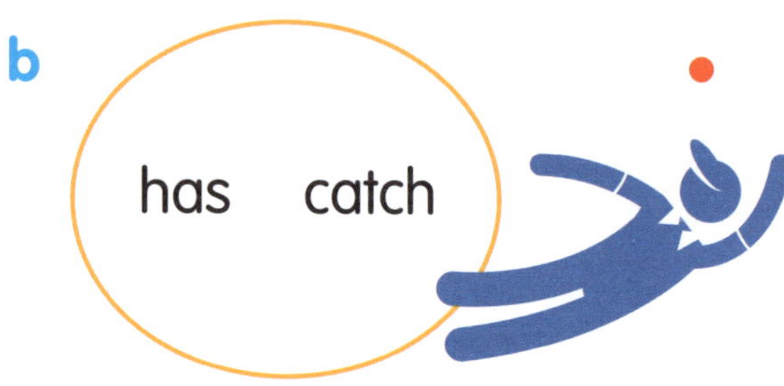

2 Underline the word that is wrong. Write it correctly. 2 marks

a Last night I cook dinner. ______________

b Last week we wash our car. ______________

3 Fill in the missing punctuation. 2 marks

a Where are we going

b We are going to the beach

4 Complete each sentence with a relating verb from the box. 3 marks

am	have	is

a It ______________ very hot today.

b I ______________ excited about getting a dog.

c The pirates ______________ treasure on their ship.

Grammar

5 **Complete each sentence with a helping verb.** 2 marks

am
are

a I __________ putting away my books.

b The children __________ cheering for their team.

6 **Cross out the word that is wrong. Write it correctly.** 2 marks

a I were waiting for the bus. __________

b Jack are eating his sandwiches. __________

7 **Fill in the missing verbs in these future tense sentences.** 2 marks

a You __________ fall if you're not careful.

b I __________ going to buy tickets for the concert.

8 **Use an adverb to complete each sentence.** 3 marks

a Elsie arrived __________ for the game.

b Come here __________ . You must see this!

c The plane glided __________ through the sky.

9 **Fill in the missing punctuation.** 2 marks

a How good was that book

b I'd like to read that book again

Dolphins and Porpoises

Read the passage and then use the comprehension skills you have learned to answer the questions.

There are 31 species of dolphin and six species of porpoise.

Some dolphin species, such as the bottlenose dolphin, live in oceans. Others live in coastal waters and rivers. Porpoises, such as the harbour porpoise, live in coastal waters.

Dolphins and porpoises eat fish and squid. They breathe through a blowhole, which closes when the animal is underwater. They have flippers and streamlined bodies. All dolphins and porpoises have a dorsal fin, except the finless porpoise.

Dolphins and porpoises mostly live and hunt in groups called pods. Pods protect dolphins from predators. If a shark attacks, bottlenose dolphins fiercely defend their pod. They ram the shark's soft belly with their snouts.

1. How many species of dolphin are there? 1 mark — LITERAL

   a thirty-six b thirty-one c thirteen d thirty

2. Where do dolphins and porpoises live? 1 mark — LITERAL

   a on land b underground

   c in water d on the land and in water

Dolphins and Porpoises

3 What helps dolphins and porpoises swim fast? 1 mark — INFERENTIAL

a their flippers and streamlined bodies
b their blowholes
c their dorsal fins
d their bottle-shaped noses

4 Which statement is true? Dolphins and porpoises eat … 1 mark — LITERAL

a seaweed and seagrass.
b sharks and whales.
c fish and squid.
d other dolphins and porpoises.

5 Where do dolphins and porpoises breathe? 1 mark — INFERENTIAL

a below the surface of the water
b above the surface of the water
c deep underwater
d on rocks and beaches

6 What is a group of dolphins called? 1 mark — LITERAL

a a herd
b a flock
c an army
d a pod

7 Which animals prey on dolphins and porpoises? 1 mark — LITERAL

a turtles
b seals
c sharks
d clown fish

8 Which word in the text shows that dolphins can be aggressive? — VOCABULARY

a fiercely
b protect
c defend
d finless

9 In the text, which words can be used in place of *ram*? 1 mark — VOCABULARY

a push around
b squeeze hard
c pull apart
d crash into

10 Which part of the dolphin is its snout? 1 mark — INFERENTIAL

a the top of the head
b the mouth and nose
c the side of the head
d the tail

Your score: ___ / 10

Your Review 2 Scores

Spelling		Grammar		Comprehension		Total
___ / 10	+	___ / 20	+	___ / 10	=	___ / 40

Week 19 Day 1 Comprehension

Artrageous

Think marks

To understand what you are reading, you can use **special marks**. These help you see the parts you understand and any new vocabulary.

I can see this part

W

What's this word?

I understand this part

Read the passage.

Colour **who** is in the story.

Circle **what** Luke imagined.

Box **what** Sophie imagined.

Underline **what** Aunt Stella imagined.

Imagine This, Imagine That

"It's easy. One person starts imagining something that doesn't exist, say a flying car and the next person has to add to it," said Luke.

"So you could imagine a flying car shaped like a fish," said Aunt Stella.

Sophie understood. "And the flying car shaped like a fish could spray fireworks from its wheels."

Circle the correct answer.

1. **What** does Luke imagine?
   - a a flying car
   - b a fish in a flying car
   - c a flying car that can swim
   - d a fish spraying fireworks
2. **Who** is in the story?
   - a a fish, a flying car, Aunt Stella
   - b Aunt Stella, Luke, Sophie
   - c a fish named Fireworks, Aunt Sophie, a car
   - d Luke, a flying car, Spray
3. **Which** word could replace *understood* in this story?
   - a hugged
   - b won
   - c proved
   - d followed

Artrageous

Read the whole story

Read the passage.

Use Think Marks to help you understand the passage.

Box **what** Sophie collected.

Circle **what** Sophie liked about the shells.

Colour what Sophie liked best.

Art Eyes

"Look out for colours, patterns, shapes, textures and shadows that catch your attention. Draw them in your journal and collect as much treasure as you can!" Aunt Stella cried.

Sophie liked the shapes and colours of the shells. She collected lots of shells of all shapes, sizes, colours and patterns.

Sophie also rubbed some rock textures into her journal and drew a rough sketch of the beach. But her most precious find was a piece of blue, weathered glass.

1. **What** did Sophie collect? ______________________
2. **What** did Sophie draw? ______________________
3. **Which** word helps you understand that Sophie *valued* the piece of glass?

   ____
4. Write about a time you found something precious.

   ____

   ____

   ____

   ____

Suffixes: er, est

When we compare two nouns, we often add the **suffix er** to an adjective; e.g., short**er**. When we compare MORE than two nouns, we often add the **suffix est** to an adjective; e.g., loud**est**.

1 Copy each list word.

paler ______	neatest ______	prouder ______
duller ______	cuter ______	steeper ______
nicer ______	newest ______	fullest ______
fewer ______	whiter ______	sharper ______
finest ______	coldest ______	smallest ______
later ______	thickest ______	clearest ______
loudest ______	fresher ______	

2 Sort the list words.

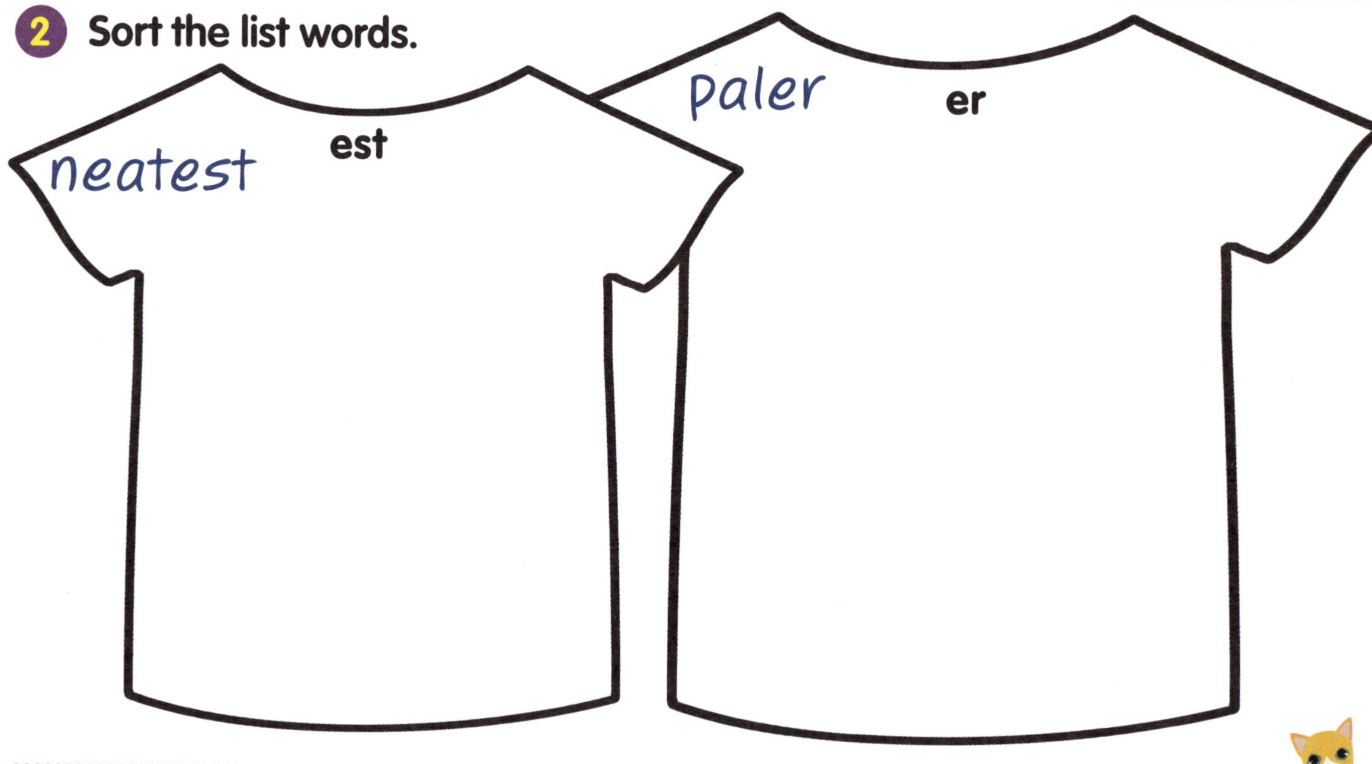

3 Underline the spelling mistake. Write the word correctly.

a Kay chose the smalest kitten from the litter. ______

b I think my puppy is cooter than my dog. ______

c The mountain was a lot steper than the hill. ______

Suffixes: er, est

1 **Match these list words to their word shapes.**

neatest fresher paler sharper nicer

a

b

c

d

e

Challenge words

2 **Copy each challenge word.**

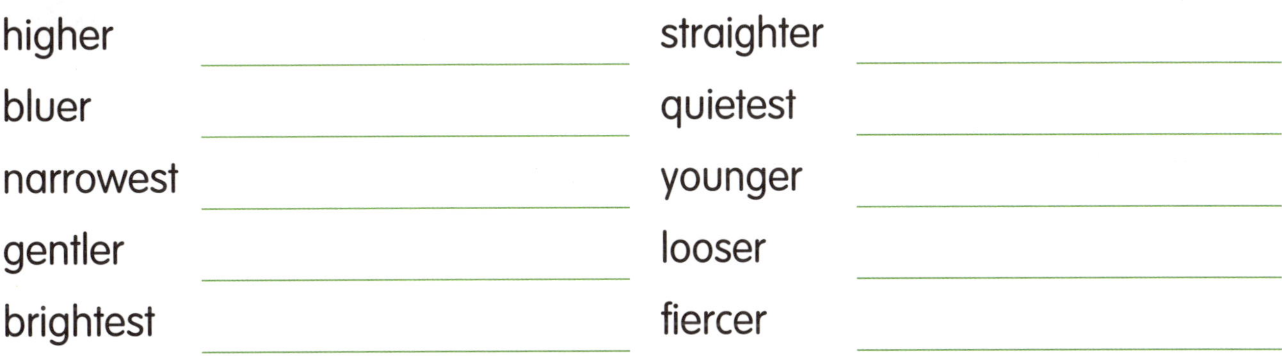

higher	straighter
bluer	quietest
narrowest	younger
gentler	looser
brightest	fiercer

3 **Colour the correct word.**

a I am [youngest] [younger] than my brother.

b The sun is [brightst] [brightest] at midday.

c Her hair is a lot [straighter] [straightest] than my hair.

d The [fiercer] [fierceer] warrior won the duel.

e The blue bird was [higher] [highest] than the orange bird.

4 **Use as many challenge words as possible to make silly sentences.**

Possessive nouns

Apostrophes (') can be used to show **ownership**. If something belongs to someone or something, the name of the owner is followed by **'s**; e.g., That is Jack**'s** pet rabbit.

1 Circle the possessive noun.

a the cat's fur
b the bird's wings
c Ruby's pencil
d Liam's jacket
e the baby's toy
f the book's cover
g Sam's pencil
h the frog's legs
i Mandy's party
j the monkey's tail

2 In each pair, [✔] the sentence that has the correct punctuation.

a My mother's purse is on the table. [ ]
b My mothers' purse is on the table. [ ]

c The birds nest is on the branch. [ ]
d The bird's nest is on the branch. [ ]

e My rabbit's fur is very soft. [ ]
f My rabbits fur is very soft. [ ]

3 Fill in the missing apostrophes.

a Alex is wearing Joses goggles.
b Dads car is in the garage.
c My grandpas glasses are on the table.
d The boys lunch is in his bag.
e The childs T-shirt is covered in mud.
f Bens kitten is very playful.

Week 20 Day 1 Comprehension

The World's Longest Toenail

Making inferences

Use **clues** in the text to make an inference.

The clues help you find the answers that are hiding in the text.

Read the passage.

Circle who was trapped.

Underline what trapped the person.

Box what the people were doing.

Colour how Jake felt.

Smelly and Stuck

Jake's toenail went PING! Jake spun around like a corkscrew. And there he stuck.

Everybody pushed and shoved. People with cameras took photos. People with notebooks asked questions.

"What does it feel like to be trapped by your toenail, Jake? they asked.

The sacks were full of fertiliser. The longest toenail in the world was no fun anymore.

Circle the correct answer.

1. **Which** best describes how Jake was feeling?
   a confused b unhappy c giddy d happy

2. Which **clue** tells you this?
   a "What does it feel like to be trapped by your toenail, Jake?"
   b The sacks were full of fertiliser.
   c The longest toenail in the world was no fun anymore.

3. What **inference** can we make about Jake?
   a Jake is the centre of attention.
   b Jake wants the longest toenail in the world.
   c Jake likes having his photo taken.

4. What **inference** can we make about the situation?
   a There were a few people there. b There were a lot of people there.
   c There was one person there.

The World's Longest Toenail

Read the whole story

Read the passage.

Circle **what** was growing.

Colour **where** the toenail grew.

Sam's Cool Idea

The longest toenail in the world was growing.

Longer and wider and taller! And it was growing FAST!

It curled three times round his body. It shot past his ears. It twisted over his head. It snaked up past the diving board.

Jake gasped as his toenail snaked and grew. As big as himself ... as tall as a tree ... as big as a house ... as tall as a crane.

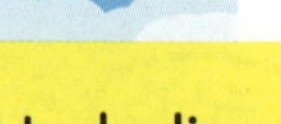

Underline the speed of Jake's growing toenail.

1. **Draw** Jake's enormous toenail.

2. How would you **feel** about having a very long toenail?

3. We can **infer** that Jake was worried. What is the clue?

Homophones

Homophones are words that sound the same but are spelled differently and have different meanings; e.g., toe, tow.

1 Copy each list word.

sale ______	steal ______	sight ______
sail ______	flee ______	site ______
meet ______	flea ______	toe ______
meat ______	hole ______	tow ______
plane ______	whole ______	rain ______
plain ______	pray ______	rein ______
steel ______	prey ______	

2 Circle the right word.

a flea / flee	b hole / whole	c tow / toe
d plane / plain	e sail / sale	f rein / rain
g meet / meat	h steel / steal	

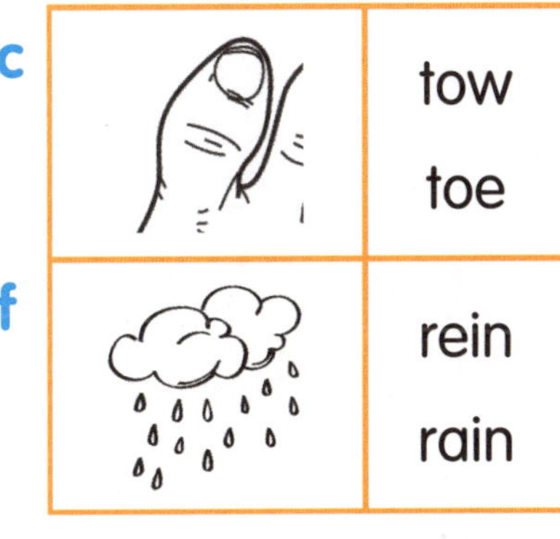

3 Write the missing word.

a The __________ landed safely at the airport.

b The wombat dug a deep ________ in the dirt.

c We watched the boats ________ past the harbour.

d I bought a box of old toys at the garage ________.

e My brother tried to __________ my new game.

Homophones

1 Which list word means?

a a tiny jumping insect that bites ____________

b all of; entire ____________

c a hard, strong metal ____________

d to run away or escape ____________

e an animal that is hunted by another ____________

Challenge words

2 Copy each challenge word.

wear	____________	haul	____________
where	____________	rays	____________
hire	____________	raise	____________
higher	____________	morning	____________
hall	____________	mourning	____________

3 Colour the correct word.

a I eat breakfast in the [morning] [mourning].

b We enjoyed the warmth of the sun's [raise] [rays].

c We climbed [higher] [hire] up the tree.

d There are lots of old photographs at the Town [Haul] [Hall].

e I didn't know [where] [wear] my sister was hiding.

4 Use as many challenge words as possible to make silly sentences.

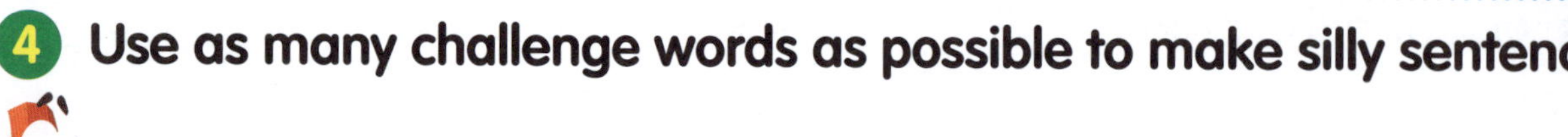

Possessive pronouns

A **pronoun** stands in place of a noun. **Possessive pronouns** show ownership or possession; e.g., That is **Mason's** bike. That is **his** bike.

1 Circle the correct possessive pronoun.

a The skateboard in the garage is (my, mine).

b The librarian gave us (ours, our) books.

c Amelia is playing with (her, hers) new game.

d Have you made (your, yours) bed yet?

e I asked (mine, my) brother to help me.

f Sarah and Lucy are helping (their, theirs) friends.

2 Complete each sentence with a pronoun from the box.

mine		their	his	your	her	ours

This is Bella's bag. It is her bag.

a That is Leo's fish. It is ______ fish.

b You have two pets. They are ______ pets.

c The car belongs to me. The car is ______.

d We have lots of pencils. The pencils are ______.

e The cards belong to Connor and Declan. They are ______ cards.

3 Circle the possessive pronouns.

a Where are my keys?

b The dog is in its kennel.

c These books are theirs.

d This hamburger is mine.

Week 21 Day 1 Comprehension

A Hairy Question

Visualisation

Good readers imagine pictures when they read a text. This is called visualising. Looking for key words in the text helps you create the images.

Read the passage.

The Home Haircut

"Easy," said Jan as she cut. "Piece of cake!"

I remember when Jan said cooking was easy. We spent an afternoon scraping burnt food off the stove.

Jan also told me that camping was easy. The tent fell on top of us during the night.

By three o'clock on Saturday afternoon there was more hair on the bathroom floor than on my head.

Underline **what** Jan said about cooking.

Circle **what** happened when Jan cooked.

Box **what** Jan said about camping.

Colour **what** happened when Jan camped.

Circle the correct answer.

1 Which **key word** describes **what** Jan thought about cooking?

a remember b scraping c easy d more

2 Which phrase helps us **visualise** Jan's cooking?

a piece of cake b cooking was easy

c scraping burnt food off the stove d tent fell on top of us

3 How does this help the reader **see** Jan's cooking adventure? It was ...

a unsuccessful. b lots of fun.

c a great success. d tasteless.

A Hairy Question

Read the passage.

Circle **what** Jan was doing.

Colour words that **describe** Freya's new hairdo.

Underline words that describe **how** Jan **felt**.

The Home Haircut

"Look in the mirror, Freya," said Jan.

I did. There was a lot of face and not much hair.

"Is it all right?" Jan said, looking worried.

"One side is longer than the other," I said softly.

Jan cut some more. Snip. Snip. Snip.

In the mirror, I looked strange. My hair was gone. Bits stuck out all over the place.

Jan's face was white.

1. What does **Freya think** of her new hairdo? ______________________

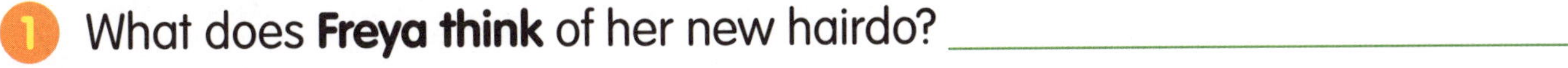

2. Which **clues** tell you? ______________________

____

3. Draw Freya and Jan's faces in the mirror.

Suffixes: ing, ed

If a verb **ends in a consonant** with a single vowel before it, **double the consonant** before adding the **suffix ing** or **ed**; e.g., tap → tapping → tapped; grab → grabbing → grabbed.

1 Copy each list word.

rubbed ______	rammed ______	grabbed ______
jogging ______	bobbing ______	stopped ______
jogged ______	tipped ______	trapping ______
wagging ______	thinned ______	blotted ______
sagged ______	planned ______	skinned ______
sipped ______	stabbed ______	flopped ______
stopping ______	gripping ______	

2 Sort the list words.

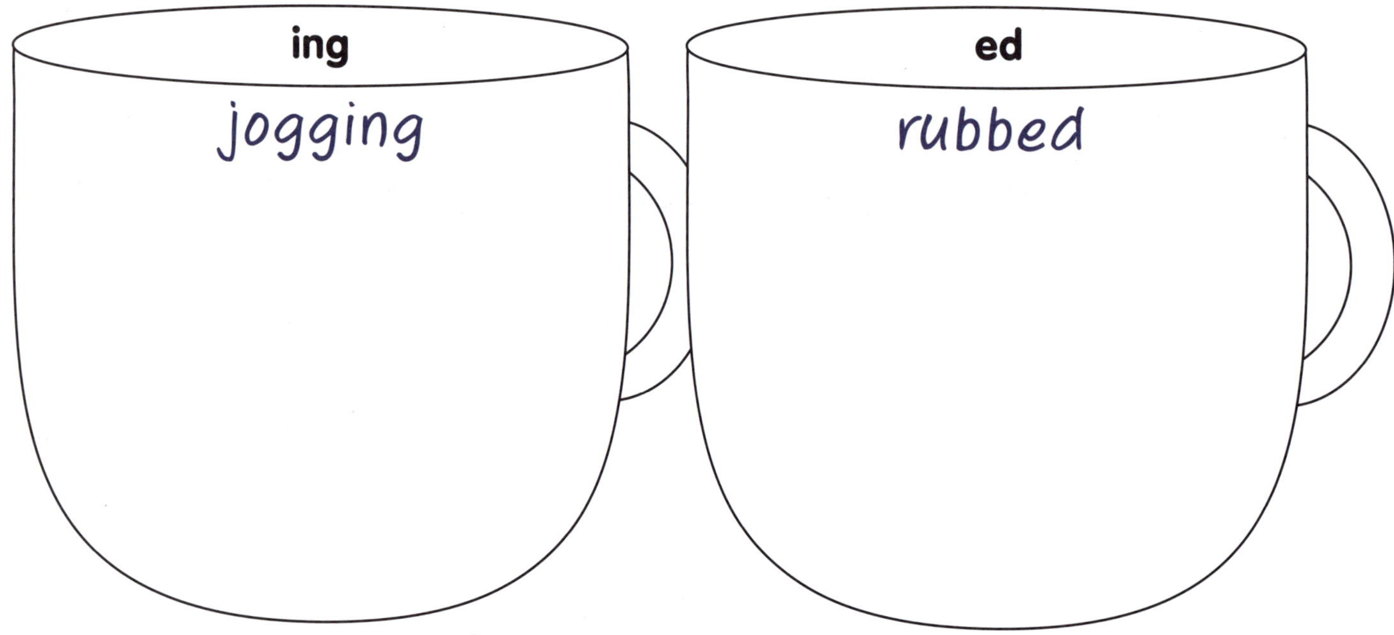

3 Complete each sentence with a list word.

a The football team is ______________ around the field.

b Yesterday, the soccer team ______________ around the field.

c I ______________ the monkey bars tightly so I wouldn't fall.

d The boats are ______________ on the water.

Suffixes: ing, ed

Challenge words

1 Copy each challenge word.

prodding ____________________
stunned ____________________
scanning ____________________
shipped ____________________
knitting ____________________
throbbed ____________________
strapping ____________________
shrugged ____________________
scrubbing ____________________
squatted ____________________

2 Colour the correct word.

a We [shiped] [shipped] the package across the country.
b Grandma is [knitting] [kniting] a big woolly jumper.
c My knee [throbbed] [throbed] with pain after I fell over.
d I was [stuned] [stunned] when my painting was chosen.
e She [squatted] [squated] down beside me to take a closer look.

3 Find the hidden challenge word.

a sdjfscanningsggf ____________________
b dfsshruggedgvsf ____________________
c dgvsscrubbingdfj ____________________
d sdfstrappingdfdfs ____________________
e ersproddinggfdre ____________________

Saying verbs

Saying verbs show different ways of saying things; e.g., **whisper**, **yell**, **mumble**, **mutter**. They are a type of **action verb**.

1 Underline the saying verb.

a "What are you doing?" asked Kyle.

b "I'm packing my sleeping bag," replied Sophia.

c "What a huge spider!" exclaimed Sarah.

d "Keep it away from me!" shrieked Ryan.

e "I've hurt my knee," sobbed Erin.

f "I don't know where my keys are," grumbled Grandpa.

g "Watch out!" yelled the man riding behind me.

2 Complete each sentence with a verb from the box.

greeted	complained	warned	cheered
whispered	begged	gasped	

a "You gave me a fright!" ______________________ Maria.

b "Hooray! We've won!" ______________________ the children.

c "Good morning, Mr Mendoza," ______________________ Joey.

d "Please may I have another slice of pizza," ______________________ Ethan.

e "You should take better care of your teeth," ______________________ the dentist.

f "Nobody ever listens to me," ______________________ Harry.

g "We mustn't let them hear us," ______________________ Ella.

Can I Join the Circus?

Finding the main idea

The main idea of a text is its key point. Details in the text help you find the main idea.

This is part of a script. It is designed to be performed by different people.

Read the passage.

Colour **who** is scared.

Underline **why** he is scared.

Box **who** is crying.

Ringmaster Roy: Chuckles, perhaps you could teach Snoz about being a clown.

Narrator: Chuckles had a great time dressing Snoz and painting him with make-up. But when Snoz saw himself in the mirror, he hid under the table.

Snoz: Not funny! Too scary! Snoz is scared!

Narrator: Snoz began to cry. Seeing a Snozalot cry made Chuckles cry too.

Chuckles: (sobbing) That is the saddest thing I have ever seen. A sobbing Snozalot!

Circle the correct answer/s.

1. Find the **main idea** of the text.
   - a Snoz is scared of himself as a clown.
   - b Chuckles is a clown.
   - c Clowns make people laugh.
   - d Snoz can't wait to join the circus.

2. Which two sentences **support** the main idea?
   - a Chuckles had a great time dressing Snoz and painting him with make-up.
   - b But when Snoz saw himself in the mirror, he hid under the table.
   - c Snoz began to cry.
   - d Seeing a Snozalot cry made Chuckles cry too.

Can I Join the Circus?

Read the passage.

the things Snoz **cannot** do.

what Bendy Betty says about Snoz.

Underline **what** Chuckles says about Snoz.

Colour what Max Manyhands says about Snoz.

Ringmaster Roy: Tell me troupe, what can Snoz the Snozalot Monster do?

Chuckles: I will tell you what he cannot do. He cannot make you laugh.

Bendy Betty: He cannot bend.

Max Manyhands: He cannot juggle.

Ringmaster Roy: I see, I see, I see. And I know he can't fly through the air.

Chuckles: He's a nice monster.

Bendy Betty: A lovely monster, really.

Max Manyhands: But Snoz has no place in Circus Bizurkus.

1 **Fill in the missing words.**

The main idea of the text is that ______________ does not belong in ______________.

2 Which **two details** helped you find the main idea?

a Everyone says Snoz can't ______________

b Max Manyhands says Snoz has ______________

Week 22 Day 3 Spelling

The k sound: k, ck

Two letters that make a single sound are called a **digraph**. The **letters ck** make the **single sound k**. When the **k sound** **comes after a single vowel**, it is usually **spelled ck**; e.g., fre**ck**le. **After a vowel digraph or a consonant**, it is **spelled k**; e.g., lea**k**, bas**k**et.

1 Copy each list word.

beak ______	luck ______	mask ______
bank ______	dusk ______	stick ______
lock ______	peck ______	shack ______
tank ______	track ______	stock ______
rock ______	pluck ______	speak ______
pink ______	cheek ______	trunk ______
tick ______	check ______	

2 Write the name for each.

a 

b 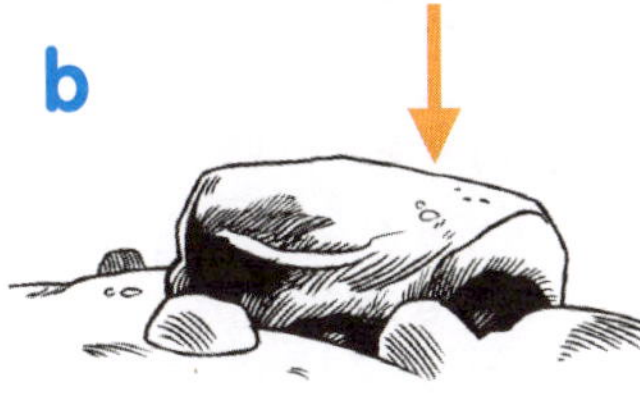

c 

d 

b ______ r ______ m ______ t ______

3 Sort the list words.

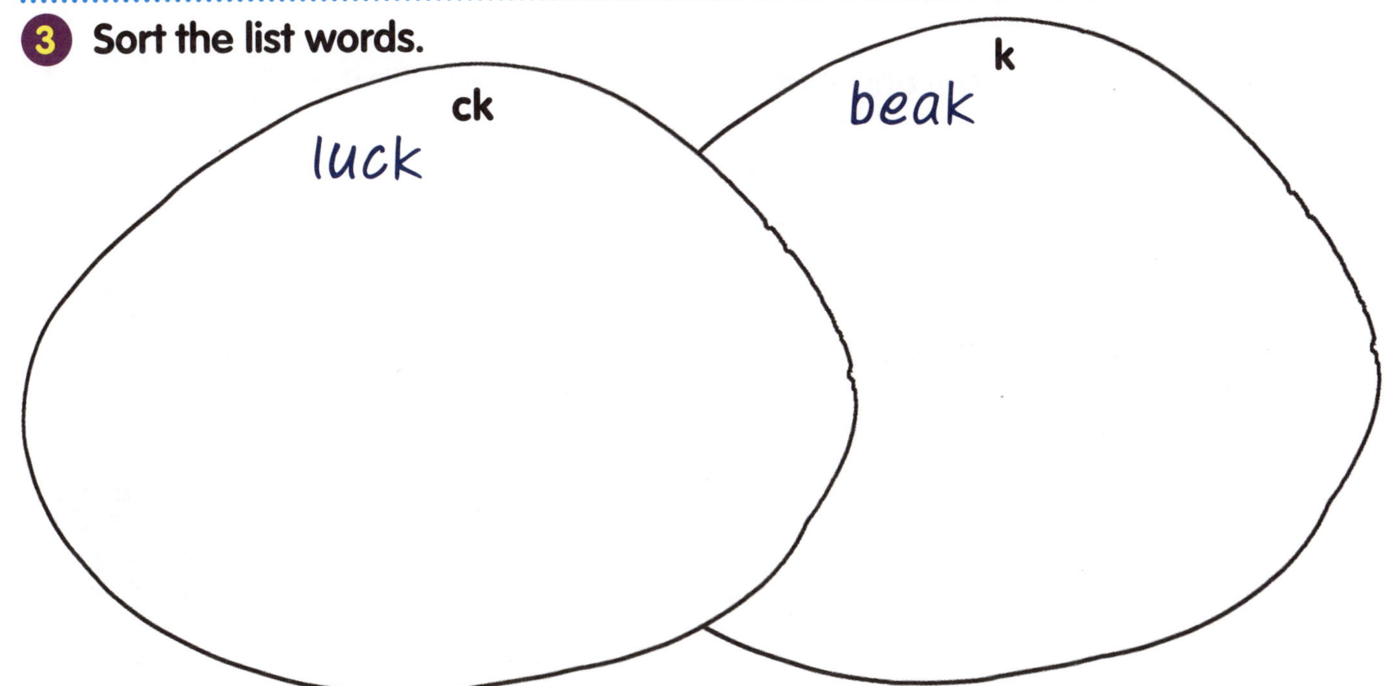

The k sound: k, ck

1 Which list word matches the clue?

a a place to save and borrow money ______

b the colour of a flamingo ______

c the time of day just before night ______

Challenge words

2 Copy each challenge word.

soak ______ stork ______

cloak ______ struck ______

thank ______ attack ______

crook ______ wreck ______

streak ______ chipmunk ______

3 Answer the question with a challenge word.

a What does a magician wear? ______

b What bird has very long legs? ______

c What animal is similar to a squirrel? ______

d What's another word for thief? ______

4 Complete each sentence with a challenge word.

a I like to ______ in a hot bath after a long day.

b I made sure to ______ her for my birthday present.

c She took off her ______ and hung it up.

d The ______ was collecting nuts for the winter.

Direct speech

Direct speech repeats the exact words someone says. **Quotation marks (" ")** are placed around the speaker's words, including any punctuation; e.g., **"**Where are you going**?"** asked Lola.

1 Underline the speaker's exact words.

a "How many pets have you got?" asked Abigail.

b "I'll wait for you outside," said Owen.

c "How good was that!" exclaimed Lily.

d "Come here at once!" shouted the angry man.

e "I wish I had a pet guinea pig," sighed the little girl.

f "Now, what have I done with my purse?" mumbled Grandma.

2 Fill in the missing quotation marks.

a How are you feeling today? asked the doctor.

b I would like porridge for breakfast, said the child.

c What a large bear! gasped Victoria.

d Don't go too near the edge, warned the ranger.

e I will never do that again, promised Ethan.

3 Write an answer. Don't forget to use quotation marks.

"How old are you, Adam?" asked Sam.

_______________________________________ said Adam.

The Lion and the Gnat

Finding the main idea

The main idea of a text is its key point. It sums up what the text is about.

Details in the text help you find the main idea.

Read the passage.

Circle the gnat's **actions**.

Underline the lion's **actions**.

Box words that describe the lion's **feelings**.

The gnat dived at the lion and stung him on the nose. The lion was furious! He swiped at the gnat but only ended up scratching himself with his sharp claws. The gnat attacked the lion again and again and the lion raged.

Circle the correct answer/s.

1. Which **best** describes the main idea of the text?
   - a A lion attacked a gnat.
   - b A lion fell down.
   - c A gnat wanted to be a lion.
   - d A gnat attacked a lion.
2. Which **two** details **support** the main idea?
   - a The gnat dived at the lion and stung him on the nose.
   - b The lion was furious!
   - c He swiped at the gnat.
   - d The lion scratched himself with his sharp claws.
   - e The gnat attacked the lion again and again and the lion raged.
3. Which **best** describes the gnat's actions?
   - a selfish
   - b kind
   - c gentle
   - d vicious

The Lion and the Gnat

Read the passage.

Underline what the lion does.

Colour what the gnat does.

Finally, the lion was worn out. He was dripping with blood from his own scratches and he lay down, defeated by the gnat. The gnat buzzed away to tell the whole Animal Kingdom about his victory over the lion but instead he flew straight into a spider's web.

1. What is the **main idea** of the text?
   - **a** A gnat flew into a spider's web.
   - **b** The smaller creature proved to be the more dangerous.

2. Which **two details** helped you find the main idea?
   - **a** The lion was ______________________
   - **b** The gnat had ______________________

3. What is the **message** from this fable? ______________________

Suffix: ly

Adding the **suffix ly** to an adjective turns it into an adverb; e.g., quick**ly**.
If the adjective **ends in y**, change the **y to i** before adding **ly**; e.g., happy → happ**ily**.

1 Copy each list word.

badly ______	mainly ______	largely ______
slowly ______	softly ______	swiftly ______
nicely ______	clearly ______	gently ______
suddenly ______	quickly ______	firmly ______
mostly ______	happily ______	quietly ______
strongly ______	easily ______	fairly ______
shyly ______	calmly ______	

2 Use list words to complete the table.

	bad	badly
a	quick	
b	strong	
c	most	
d	nice	

3 Underline the spelling mistake. Write the word correctly.

a I jumped easly over the low fence. ______

b I quikly ate my dinner so I could play outside. ______

c We spoke sofly so we didn't wake our parents. ______

d I sudenly had a brilliant idea. ______

e The turtle crawled slowlee up the beach. ______

Suffix: ly

1 Write the list words in alphabetical order.

______ ______ ______ ______

______ ______ ______ ______

______ ______ ______ ______

______ ______ ______ ______

______ ______ ______ ______

Challenge words

2 Copy each challenge word.

extremely	______	completely	______
actually	______	differently	______
finally	______	surely	______
slightly	______	absolutely	______
normally	______	equally	______

3 Colour the correct word.

a Mum shared the sushi [eqwually] [equally] between us.

b I [finaly] [finally] finished writing my story.

c We went in [completly] [completely] different directions.

d I am [slightly] [sleightly] taller than my brother.

4 Use as many challenge words as possible to make a silly sentence.

______

______

______

Questions and exclamations

Questions end with a **question mark (?)**. Exclamations end with an **exclamation mark (!)**. Exclamation phrases and sentences show surprise or excitement. Words or phrases that show strong feelings can also end in exclamation marks; e.g., How scary! Ouch!

1 Read the following sentences and then [✔] the answer to the question.

How good was that pie!

How good was that pie?

Did the punctuation make you read the sentences differently?

☐ Yes ☐ No

2 Fill in the missing punctuation.

a What a fluffy tail that cat has ☐

b What does this word mean ☐

c How many pencils are there in the box ☐

d How exciting was that ☐

e Who gave you those cards ☐

3 Use the pictures to help you write questions.

Dinosaur Dig

Sequencing events

To find the sequence of events in a text, look at numbers and words that give clues to the order in which things happen.

Read the passage.

Circle **where** you might find fossils.

Box **what** the bones are removed from.

Finding Fossils

Places where rocks are eroding might have fossils. Creek banks, dry riverbeds and cliff faces are all good places to look. Most fossils are covered by a thick layer of rock. At some sites, explosives blow up the rock and bulldozers cart it away. Often the whole block of rock, with its bones, is cut out. This is taken back to the lab where the bones are carefully removed.

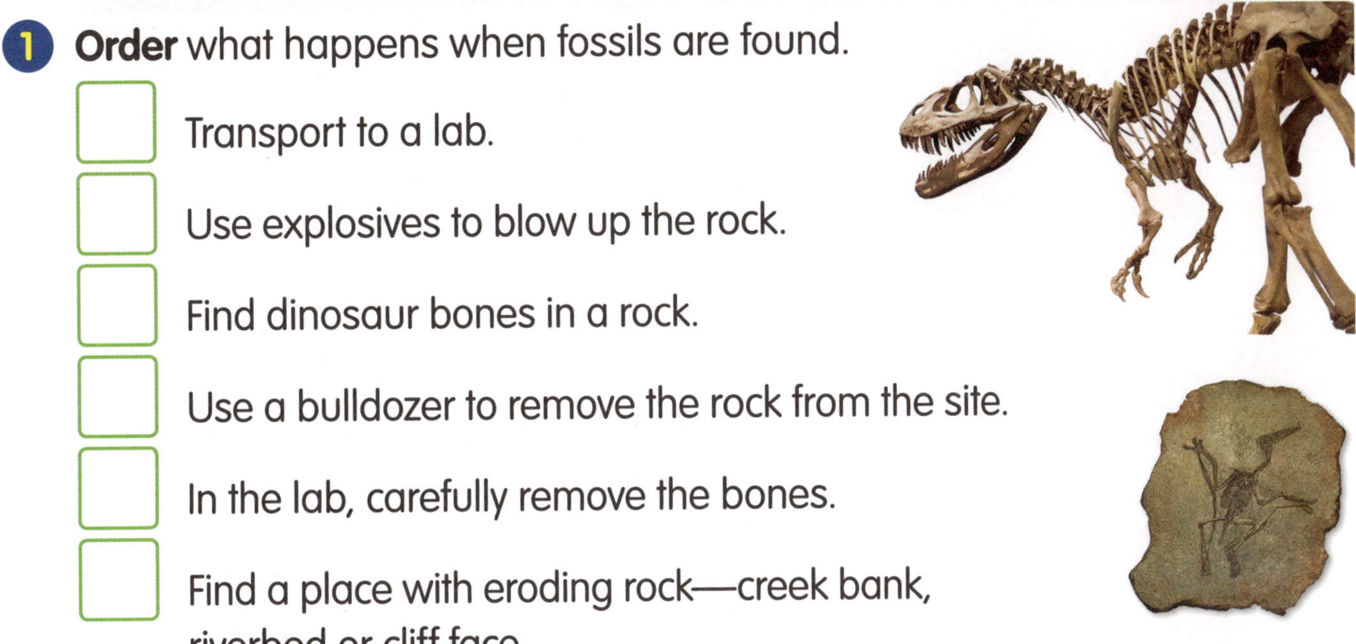

1. **Order** what happens when fossils are found.
   - ☐ Transport to a lab.
   - ☐ Use explosives to blow up the rock.
   - ☐ Find dinosaur bones in a rock.
   - ☐ Use a bulldozer to remove the rock from the site.
   - ☐ In the lab, carefully remove the bones.
   - ☐ Find a place with eroding rock—creek bank, riverbed or cliff face.
2. After this, **where** might children view the fossils? ______________________

Dinosaur Dig

Read the full text

Read the passage.

Underline the **first step** in putting a dinosaur back together.

Colour how the skeleton is put back together.

what happens after photos are taken and drawings made.

Giant Jigsaw Puzzles

Putting a dinosaur back together takes skill, patience and a lot of time.

Using photos and drawings, the skeleton is laid out on the floor and then put back together from the ground up.

Most bones are too fragile to become a skeleton in a museum. A plaster or plastic cast is made. It is rare to find a complete skeleton—most museums' dinosaurs are put together with extra parts.

1 **Draw** the process of putting together dinosaur skeletons.

Step 1	Step 2
Step 3	Step 4

Week 24 Day 3 Spelling

Endings: dge, ge

At the end of a word or syllable, the **j sound** is either spelled **dge** or **ge**; e.g., bri**dge**, oran**ge**.

1 Copy each list word.

age ______	hedge ______	strange ______
edge ______	fudge ______	change ______
huge ______	wedge ______	fringe ______
village ______	bridge ______	smudge ______
badge ______	image ______	garage ______
large ______	orange ______	plunge ______
judge ______	charge ______	

2 Write the name for each.

a

b ______

b

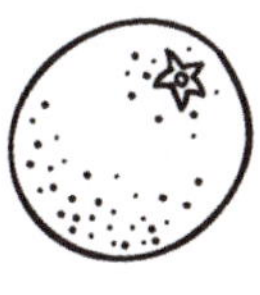

o ______

c

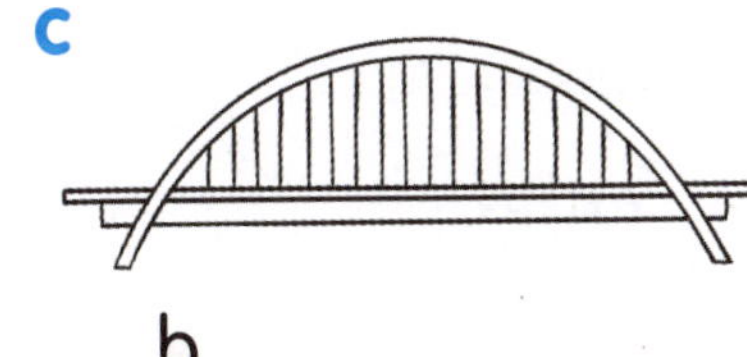

b ______

d

h ______

e

j ______

3 Which list word means?

a a dirty mark or stain ______

b unusual or odd ______

c a picture of something ______

d a round, juicy fruit ______

e a row of bushes used as a fence ______

Endings: dge, ge

1 Unscramble the letters to make a list word.

a ungple ______
b ngecha ______
c ingefr ______
d agevill ______
e rgecha ______
f raggae ______

Challenge words

2 Copy each challenge word.

bulge ______
partridge ______
cottage ______
sausage ______
package ______
damage ______
passage ______
manage ______
cringe ______
courage ______

3 Which challenge word means?

a a small house ______
b a wrapped object ______
c the ability to face your fears ______
d a plump bird with brown or grey feathers ______
e can be cooked on a barbecue ______

4 Colour the correct word.

a We apologised for the damage damadge we did to the garden.
b We could see a light at the end of the dark passadge passage.
c I walked to the post office to collect my package packadge.

Sequencing adverbs

Adverbs give information about **verbs**. **Sequencing adverbs** show **when** or **how often** something happens; e.g., We visited our friend **yesterday**.

1 Complete each sentence with an adverb.

weekly
tomorrow
already
later
always

a I ________________ eat my vegetables.

b I have ________________ seen that movie.

c I hope to finish this book by ________________.

d You can finish your game ________________.

e The comic comes out ________________.

2 Circle the sequencing adverbs.

a The clock strikes hourly.

b I brush my teeth regularly.

c I have never eaten a snail!

d I saw her in the library earlier.

e The coach wants to see us now.

f I sometimes forget to brush my teeth.

g We're going to watch the football game tonight.

3 Complete the following sentence.

Yesterday I ____

____

____

Inventing the Future

Finding facts and information
To find facts and information in a text, ask the questions **Who? What? Where?** or **When?** The answers can be clearly seen in the text.

Read the passage.

A World-changing Gizmo

It all began in 1947. That's when three scientists invented the transistor. The three scientists were from the Bell Laboratories. Their names were John Bardeen, Walter Brattain and William Shockley.

The first transistor was about the size of your thumb. It was made from a paperclip, gold foil, wire and a bit of plastic. Transistors were first used in telephones.

Transistors are in computers, the Internet, mobile phones, TVs, video cameras, calculators, hand-held games, radar, satellites and night vision technology.

Circle **who** invented the transistor.

Underline **when** the first transistor was made.

Box **what** the first transistors were made from.

Colour **where** transistors were first used.

Circle the correct answer.

1. **What** was the occupation of the inventors?
   a teachers b physiotherapists c scientists d professors

2. **What** size was the first transistor?
   a paperclip-sized b thumb-sized
   c mobile phone-sized d telephone-sized

3. **Where** are transistors used today?
   a paperclips b mobile phones c plastic d your thumb

Inventing the Future

Read the full text: *Inventing the Future*

Read the passage.

Highlight what Dr Nakamatsu holds the world record for.

Underline what Dr Nakamatsu invented.

Box when Dr Nakamatsu likes inventing.

Colour where Dr Nakamatsu invents.

Why Didn't I Think of That?

Dr Nakamatsu is a modern inventor. He holds the world record for the most patents and inventions. Dr Nakamatsu has over 3200 inventions.

Dr Nakamatsu often came up with ideas underwater. He invented a notepad that he could use underwater to write down his ideas.

Dr Nakamatsu only sleeps four hours a night. He says the best time for new ideas is between midnight and 4 am. He has two special rooms that help him think.

1. **What** was Dr Nakamatsu's underwater problem?

   ____

2. **What** was Dr Nakamatsu's solution?

   ____

3. Think of a problem that you could invent a gizmo for.

Who would need it?	**What** would it be?	**Where** would it be used?	**When** would it be needed?

Week 25 Day 3 Spelling

Compound words

Compound words are formed when two or more words join together to make a new word; e.g., hairbrush.

1 Copy each list word.

armpit ________	windmill ________	eyebrow ________
pancake ________	raincoat ________	handshake ________
freeway ________	snowman ________	rainfall ________
starfish ________	backpack ________	leftovers ________
shoelace ________	grandchild ________	teardrop ________
anybody ________	hairbrush ________	strawberry ________
uphill ________	driveway ________	

2 Add the pictures to make a list word.

Compound words

1 Underline the spelling mistake. Write the word correctly.

a Strawbery is my favourite flavour of ice cream. ______

b In winter we like to go outside and build a snoman. ______

c On rainy days I pack my umbrella and raincote. ______

d I packed my hat and sunscreen into my bakpack. ______

e I couldn't find my harebrush, so I had to use my comb. ______

Challenge words

2 Copy each challenge word.

outdoors	______	background	______
marketplace	______	doughnut	______
elsewhere	______	clockwork	______
downstairs	______	earphone	______
watermelon	______	cheeseburger	______

3 Complete each sentence with a challenge word.

a When I eat ______ I always spit out the black seeds.

b Dad told us to go and play ______.

c We brought home a huge box of peaches from the ______.

d I wanted the ______ with pink icing and sprinkles.

4 Which challenge word means?

a a large fruit with green skin ______

b describes something running smoothly ______

Noun groups

A **noun group** is built around a noun. It can include **articles**, (a, an, the), **pronouns** (my, his, her) and **adjectives** (small, new, red); e.g., a cheese pizza, his silver helmet.

1 Circle the noun in each phrase.

a a new barbecue

b my red umbrella

c the sweet lolly

d an old man

e her big truck

f two little mice

g a rainy day

h a blue bat

i an oval shape

2 Complete each sentence with an adjective from the box.

tiny	electric	fluffy	dirty	new	juicy

a My friend has a ________________ white cat.

b He is eating a soft, ________________ peach.

c His boat has an ________________ motor.

d I watched the ________________ ant crawl up the wall.

e My friend let me ride his ________________ bike.

f She removed the ________________ mark from her shirt.

Boats

Compare and contrast
Compare and contrast information by looking for the **similarities** and **differences**.

Read the passage.

Moving People

People travel short distances on ferries. Cruise ships can take you all the way around the world.

Ferries travel across rivers, harbours and lakes. Some people catch ferries to work or school. Larger ferries also travel between islands or even between countries.

People take holidays on cruise ships. You live on the ship as it travels to different cities and countries. Cruise ships have restaurants, shops, movie theatres and bedrooms called cabins.

1. Compare and contrast everyday boats we use. Tick [✔] the correct answers on the table.

	Travels on and between					Travel for			Time spent on board		On board		
	rivers	harbours	lakes	cities	countries	work	holiday	school	minutes or hours	days or weeks	shops	movie theatres	bathrooms
ferry													
cruise ship													

Use the information in the table to answer the questions below.

2. What would you find on **both** ferries and cruise ships?

____

3. Between which two places do both ferries and cruise ships travel?

____

Boats

Read the passage.

The Navy

Destroyers, submarines and aircraft carriers are all used by the navy.

Destroyers are fast. They are often used to protect bigger, slower ships. They can hold up to 300 people.

Submarines travel under the water. They hold up to 150 people and can move quickly if they must.

Aircraft carriers are the biggest ships in the navy. They carry planes which can take off and land on their long decks. They can have up to 5000 sailors and pilots on board at any one time.

1 Complete the table.

Boat	What does it do?	How many people can it hold?	Interesting fact
destroyer			
submarine			
aircraft carrier			

2 **How** are destroyers, submarines and aircraft carriers similar?

Week 26 Day 3 Spelling

Contractions

A **contraction** is two words joined to make a shorter word. The left out letters are replaced by an **apostrophe** ('); e.g., you will → you'll.

1 Copy each list word.

I'm ________	we'll ________	hasn't ________
he's ________	don't ________	where's ________
it's ________	she'll ________	what's ________
I've ________	it'd ________	you'd ________
how's ________	who's ________	can't ________
there's ________	it'll ________	didn't ________
won't ________	who'll ________	

2 Underline the spelling mistake. Write the word correctly.

a Jay told me that h'es not coming to the party. ________

b I cant' stand on my head! ________

c Don't worry, she'l be here any minute. ________

d Im the tallest player in my basketball team. ________

e I'ts been two weeks since I've seen my friend. ________

3 Draw a line to match the words to their contractions.

has not	didn't
a where is	hasn't
b did not	how's
c I have	where's
d how is	I've

Contractions

1 Rewrite the contraction correctly.

a itll ______ b well ______

c wont ______ d youd ______

Challenge words

2 Copy each challenge word.

wasn't ______ haven't ______

they've ______ doesn't ______

you're ______ o'clock ______

mustn't ______ couldn't ______

weren't ______ would've ______

3 Write the matching contraction.

a were not ______ b would have ______

c does not ______ d was not ______

e could not ______ f you are ______

4 Colour the correct word.

a I [wasn't] [wan'st] sure which direction we should take.

b You [musun't] [mustn't] make a sound or you'll wake the baby.

c I [couldn't] [could't] go to football training because I felt unwell.

d The hike starts promptly at nine [o'clock] [oclock].

Conjunctions

A **conjunction** joins single words in sentences; e.g, Alex **and** Isabella are twins. It also joins parts of a sentence; e.g., I bought a hamburger **but** I didn't eat it.

1 Complete each sentence with a conjunction from the box. Use each conjunction once.

so
but
nor
or
and

a I Ask either Lucy __________ Sarah to help you.

b I eat lots of fruit __________ vegetables.

c I was feeling sick __________ I stayed in bed.

d I don't like spinach, __________ do I like broccoli.

e I switched on the engine, __________ nothing happened.

2 Circle the correct word.

a There were men, women (nor, and, but) children at the concert.

b I haven't cleaned my teeth, (but, or, nor) have I brushed my hair.

c It was cold, (but, or, so) I put on a jacket.

d The bus was full (or, nor, so) I waited for the next one.

e You can have a milkshake (or, but, so) an ice cream (or, so, but) you can't have both.

3 Write endings for the following sentences.

a I like apples and __________________________.

b I looked under my bed but __________________________

__________________________.

c We can go to the park, or __________________________

__________________________.

Mammals

Making inferences

Use **clues** in the text to make an inference.

The clues help you find the answers that are hiding in the text.

Read the passage.

the **hoofed animals.**

Underline the **collective noun.**

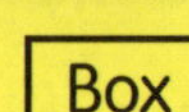

two verbs that tell what baby elephants do.

Hoofed Mammals

Hoofed mammals eat plants. They are herbivores. Zebras, giraffes and elephants are all hoofed mammals.

Many hoofed mammals live in groups called herds. They often live on open plains or grasslands. The herd moves from place to place in search of food. Zebras and wildebeests live in large herds.

Elephants are the largest land animals. They live in family groups called herds. Baby elephants feed on mother's milk for two years while they grow.

Circle the correct answer.

1. Which **best** describes how hoofed animals live?
   - a in harmony with many other animals
   - b on their own
   - c in pairs
   - d in large groups

2. Which **clue** tells you this?
   - a Hoofed mammals eat plants.
   - b Zebras, giraffes and elephants are all hoofed mammals.
   - c Many hoofed mammals live in groups called herds.
   - d The herd moves from place to place in search of food.
   - e Elephants are the largest land animals.

Mammals

Read the passage.

Underline the word that **compares** the **size** of apes and monkeys.

Box the word that **compares** the **size** of gorillas and other apes.

Monkeys and Apes

Monkeys and apes are mammals called primates. They are warm-blooded, furry animals that suckle their young.

Baboons, mandrills and howlers are all monkeys. Monkeys are very good climbers. They use their hands, feet and tails to help them climb.

Apes are larger than monkeys. Chimpanzees, gibbons, orangutans and gorillas are all apes. Apes do not have tails.

Gorillas are the largest of all the apes and are tailless. They live in family groups.

Colour **which** primates have tails.

Circle **which** primates don't have tails.

1 Use the information to order the size of primates.

small	larger	largest

2 What is the physical difference between monkeys and apes?

____

3 Which **clue** tells you? ______________________________

____

Week 27 Day 3 Spelling

Plurals: s, es

We can change nouns from singular to plural nouns by adding the **suffix s** or **es**; e.g., spider**s**, kiss**es**.

1 Copy each list word.

pigs	______	cages	______	classes	______
bees	______	eyes	______	flashes	______
foxes	______	lions	______	bunches	______
dishes	______	tricks	______	kisses	______
books	______	things	______	sharks	______
rocks	______	plants	______	lambs	______
coats	______	spiders	______		

2 Write the singular and plural for each word.

a		______	______	
b		______	______	
c		______	______	
d		______	______	
e		______	______	
f		______	______	
g		______	______	
h		______	______	

Plurals: s, es

1 Complete each sentence with a list word.

a There were two ______________ rolling in the mud.

b We could hear the ______________ roaring loudly outside our tent.

c I watched several ______________ buzzing noisily around the garden.

d I hung all the ______________ in the wardrobe.

e I borrowed two new ______________ from the library.

f The florist had ______________ of beautiful flowers outside her shop.

Challenge words

2 Copy each challenge word.

fingers ______________	branches ______________
flowers ______________	quizzes ______________
monkeys ______________	oranges ______________
catches ______________	giraffes ______________
watches ______________	cabbages ______________

3 Answer the question with a challenge word.

a What kinds of animals have long necks? ______________

b What do bees collect pollen from? ______________

c What do you have on your hands? ______________

d What fruit has the same name and colour? ______________

4 Complete each sentence with a challenge word.

a The ______________ sat in the tree eating bananas.

b I have five ______________ on one hand and five toes on one foot.

Contractions

A **contraction** is a shorter way of writing a word or words. To make the contraction, letters are left out. An **apostrophe (')** shows where the letters have been left out; e.g., **I will** help you. **I'll** help you.

1 Replace the underlined words with a contraction.

a She <u>has not</u> found her hockey stick. ________

b I <u>cannot</u> solve this problem. ________

c <u>I have</u> finished the apple pie. ________

d That <u>is not</u> my jumper. ________

e They <u>are not</u> at home. ________

I've
hasn't
aren't
can't
isn't

2 Which letter/s does the apostrophe replace?

we will	we'll	wi
a she is	she's	________
b they are	they're	________
c do not	don't	________
d you have	you've	________

3 Write the words correctly.

mustve	must've	a theyll	________
b didnt	________	c thats	________
d havent	________	e doesnt	________

Spelling

Use this review to test your knowledge. It has three parts—**Spelling**, **Grammar** and **Comprehension**. If you're unsure of an answer, go back and read the rules and generalisations in the blue boxes.

You have learned about:

- suffixes: er, est
- the k sound: k, ck
- compound words
- homophones
- suffix: ly
- contractions
- suffixes: ing, ed
- endings: dge, ge
- plurals: s, es

1 Complete. 2 marks

a one spider, but two ____________

b one branch, but two ____________

2 Which word completes the sentence? 1 mark

It was the ____________ winter in thirty years.

a colder b cold c coldest d colds

3 Colour the letter/s that correctly completes each word. 1 mark

a chee [ck] [k] b bri [dge] [ge]

4 Complete the contractions. 2 marks

a who is → ____________ b would have → ____________

5 Which word completes the sentence? 1 mark

Our family finished the ____________ pie.

a whole b hole c holey d wholes

6 Name the compound word. 1 mark

+ = ____________

7 Which word completes the sentence? 1 mark

My pony ____________ jumped the fence.

a easy b easily c easier d easiest

8 Underline the spelling mistake. Spell it correctly. 1 mark

I am kniting a scarf. ____________

Your score
/10

Grammar

You have learned about:

- possessive nouns
- direct speech
- noun groups
- possessive pronouns
- questions and exclamations
- conjunctions
- saying verbs
- sequencing adverbs
- contractions

1 Add the apostrophes. 2 marks

a That is Dans book.

b The babys toy is in the box.

2 Circle the correct possessive pronoun. 2 marks

a The bat is (her, hers), not (your, yours).

b (Their, Theirs) pencils are on the table and (my, mine) are in the drawer.

3 Complete each sentence with a verb from the box. 2 marks

whispered	yelled

a Rosie ______________________ at the top of her voice.

b Sid ______________________ a secret in my ear.

4 Add in the missing quotation marks. 2 marks

a How many lollies have you had? asked Joey.

b Not half as many as you, replied Ella.

Grammar

5 Complete each sentence with a conjunction from the box. Use each conjunction once. 4 marks

so	nor	or	but

a I have not visited Europe, ______________ have I travelled around the United States.

b I have eaten my lunch ______________ I am still hungry.

c I was hungry ______________ I made myself a sandwich.

d You can sit ______________ you can stand.

6 Colour the sequencing adverbs. 2 marks

a They will be here later.

b Come here immediately!

7 Underline the noun in each group. 2 marks

a two furry little squirrels

b a long wooden table

8 Fill in the missing punctuation. 2 marks

a That is weird____

b Where are my flippers____

9 Write the contractions of the underlined words. 2 marks

a <u>We will</u> help you if we can. ______________

b <u>It is</u> your turn next. ______________

Ming Ming's Adventure

Read the passage and then answer the questions.

Ming Ming lived in the village of Jizhou. She was a daydreamer. She liked to pretend she was a princess.

Her father complained that she was a lazy child but her mother said she had a good heart.

One day, Ming Ming's mother sent Ming Ming into the mountains to collect herbs. Her mother warned her to concentrate because the paths were dangerous.

Ming Ming set off. Before long, she was lost in her own imaginary world and tripped over a fallen log. She fell and smashed the special basket her mother had given her.

"Oh no!" she cried. "How will I carry the herbs home? Mother will never forgive me."

As Ming Ming wiped away her tears, she noticed some hollow seed pods nearby. She would use those to carry the herbs she collected.

When Ming Ming returned to the village, she told her parents what had happened. Her father praised his daughter for clever thinking.

1 Which country is the village of Jizhou likely to be in? 1 mark **INFERENTIAL**

a Australia b America c England d China

2 We can infer that Ming Ming didn't always do her chores. Which phrase is the clue? 1 mark **INFERENTIAL**

a a good heart b a lazy child c a quiet spot d a young girl

Ming Ming's Adventure

3 Why did Ming Ming go into the mountains? 1 mark — LITERAL

a to pick flowers
b to collect herbs
c to sit and daydream
d to look for seed pods

4 Which words best describe Ming Ming? 1 mark — CRITICAL

a lazy and cruel
b kind and imaginative
c hardworking and clever
d clumsy and sad

5 Which word is closest in meaning to *concentrate*? 1 mark — VOCABULARY

a listen
b watch
c focus
d manage

6 What happened first? 1 mark — LITERAL

a Ming Ming collected the herbs.
b The basket broke.
c Ming Ming tripped.
d Ming Ming saw the seed pods.

7 Why was Ming Ming crying? She ... 1 mark — INFERENTIAL

a was upset about the broken basket.
b hurt herself when she tripped.
c was scared of her father.
d couldn't find any herbs.

8 What is the main purpose of the text? 1 mark — CRITICAL

a to give information
b to tell a story
c to explain how something works
d to state a point of view

9 What is the main message of the text? 1 mark — LITERAL

a Respect your parents.
b Take care of other people's things.
c Every problem has a solution.
d Look where you're going.

10 Why did Ming Ming's father praise his daughter?
For her ... 1 mark — LITERAL

a honesty
b cleverness
c bravery
d hard work

Your score: ___ / 10

Your Review 3 Scores

Spelling		Grammar		Comprehension		Total
___	+	___	+	___	=	___
10		20		10		40

Computer Virus

Drawing conclusions

To draw conclusions from a text, use clues to make your own judgments.

The clues help you find the answers that are hiding in the text.

Read the passage.

Circle three verbs that show **how Vinnie moved**.

Underline Vinnie's **dialogue**.

Box a word that shows **how Vinnie's mum felt**.

Colour Mum's **dialogue**.

The Sniffles

Vinnie raced in the front door. His bag skidded across the living room floor.

"What's going on in here?" Vinnie's mum stood in the doorway, hands on her hips.

Vinnie walked over and picked up his bag.

"Sorry, Mum. I'm in a bit of a hurry."

"What about a snack?"

"I'm not hungry."

Mary stood in shock as she watched him run up the stairs.

Circle the correct answer/s.

1. Which is the best **conclusion**?

   a Vinnie was in a rush.
   b Vinnie likes doing his homework.
   c Vinnie is hungry.
   d Vinnie likes to keep things neat and tidy.

2. Which two words are **clues** to question 1's answer?

   a walked
   b raced
   c run
   d stood

3. Which is the best **conclusion**?

   a Mum is untidy and doesn't like tidying.
   b Mum doesn't like making snacks.
   c Mum was surprised Vinny didn't want a snack.
   d Vinnie was tired from a long day at school.

Computer Virus

Read the passage.

Colour words that describe **Dr Hacker's arrival**.

Box Dr Hacker's **dialogue**.

Underline Vinnie's **dialogue**.

Dr Hacker

Vinnie pulled the ad from his pocket and dialled the number.

"Hello," said the voice on the other end of the line.

"Are you Dr Hacker?" asked Vinnie.

"That's right."

Vinnie explained his problem.

"Never fear, young Vinnie. I'll be there in a flash," said Dr Hacker.

Vinnie hung up. Smoke filled the hall and a flash of light blinded him.

Dr Hacker waved away the smoke. "Show me your sick computer."

1. What can we **conclude** about Vinnie's problem?

2. From his arrival, what can we **conclude** about Dr Hacker?

3. Which **clues** tell you?

The text says, "

Irregular past tense verbs

Irregular verbs do not use the **suffix ed** in the past tense. Some irregular verbs change their spelling and sound different in the past tense; e.g., I **eat** my apple. I **ate** my apple.

1 Copy each list word.

did	______	awoke	______	forgot	______
ate	______	became	______	froze	______
fled	______	began	______	swung	______
gave	______	bound	______	flung	______
went	______	clung	______	fought	______
stole	______	sprang	______	chose	______
shook	______	knew	______		

2 Unscramble these list words.

a mecabe ______
b undbo ______
c ngaspr ______
d ghtfou ______
e ungsw ______
f okeaw ______

3 Complete the list words.

a d _ d b cl _ _ g c ch _ _ e d fr _ z _ e s _ _ l _

4 Underline the spelling mistake. Write the word correctly.

a I awake in the middle of the night. ______
b After his bath, the dog shake water everywhere. ______
c Yesterday I eat five sandwiches and two muesli bars. ______
d Mum give me some money to buy bread. ______
e I forget to pack my overdue library books. ______

Irregular past tense verbs

Challenge words

1 Copy each challenge word.

built	______	caught	______
brought	______	dealt	______
taught	______	heard	______
struck	______	meant	______
shrank	______	understood	______

2 Colour the correct word.

a I [brings] [brought] chocolate fudge brownies to the picnic.

b I [taught] [teaches] my little sister how to count to five.

c The branch [struck] [striked] me in the back of the head.

d I hope she [understood] [understand] my instructions.

e I [caught] [catch] the ball before it hit the window.

3 Which challenge word means?

a past tense of catch ______

b past tense of shrink ______

c past tense of bring ______

d past tense of strike ______

e past tense of teach ______

f past tense of build ______

Irregular past tense verbs

Past tense verbs show that an action has already happened. Some past tense verbs are formed by adding **ed** to the present form; e.g., They talk**ed**.

Irregular verbs change in other ways or do not change at all; e.g., break → broke, read → read.

1 **Draw lines to match the verbs.**

Present tense	Past tense
grow	went
a think	felt
b buy	brought
c fall	thought
d bring	grew
e go	bought
f feel	fell

2 **Write the following verbs in the past tense.**

a give ______

b eat ______

c is ______

d win ______

e steal ______

f begin ______

g has ______

3 **Write the words in the past tense to complete each sentence.**

a I (know) ______ the answer.

b We (tell) ______ them what to do.

c They (sit) ______ on the bench.

d She (writes) ______ in her book.

e The bird (flies) ______ away.

f I (see) ______ a rhino at the zoo.

g He (makes) ______ a paper hat.

h She (teaches) ______ me to read.

Game Plan

Making predictions

You can predict what is going to happen in a text based on clues in the words and pictures.

Read the passage.

Dear Sophie,

Thanks for your letter. I am sending you and your friend Luke my latest Cosmic Creature called Radiant. I would be delighted to share a few tricks of the trade with you and Luke. I will send my helicopter to pick you up at 10:15 am this Saturday, from the soccer field near your house. Bring Gizmo along too.

Don't be late. I don't like to wait.

Yours in fun,
Professor Flukelar

Circle the correct answers.

1. Which **two predictions** can you make about what will happen in the story?
   - a Luke will forget to bring Gizmo and Professor Flukelar will be angry.
   - b Sophie and Luke will spend the day with Professor Flukelar.
   - c Sophie will break her Cosmic Creature because she doesn't like it.
   - d Sophie and Luke will learn many new ideas from Professor Flukelar.

2. What **evidence** is there in the text to support your predictions?
   - a Don't be late.
   - b I am sending you and your friend Luke my latest Cosmic Creature called Radiant.
   - c I would be delighted to share a few tricks of the trade with you and Luke.
   - d Thanks for your letter.
   - e Bring Gizmo along too.

Game Plan

Read the whole story

Read the passage.

'What if ...'

"But how do you think of things like that?" asked Sophie.

"Yeah," said Luke. "How do you get to be the one who sees something in a new way, when no one else has?"

"Well," said the professor, smiling, "there are a few little tricks that I can share with you."

The professor led them into his workroom. It was lined with his wonderful creations. All the Cosmic Creatures were there, as well as his siren balls, superfast glider kits and stretchable blocks.

1. **What** will Sophie and Luke learn from Professor Flukelar?

2. Predict **one** piece of advice the professor will give Sophie and Luke.

3. Draw what a Cosmic Creature might look like.

Split digraphs

Two letters that make a single sound are called a **digraph**. When **vowel digraphs** are **separated by a consonant**, they become **split digraphs**; e.g., **ba**k**e**, **bo**n**e**, **ru**l**e**.

1 **Copy each list word.**

face ______	stone ______	prune ______
safe ______	smile ______	slide ______
nine ______	rule ______	skate ______
bone ______	alone ______	blade ______
June ______	stole ______	shade ______
these ______	glide ______	whole ______
close ______	plate ______	

2 **Write the name for each.**

a 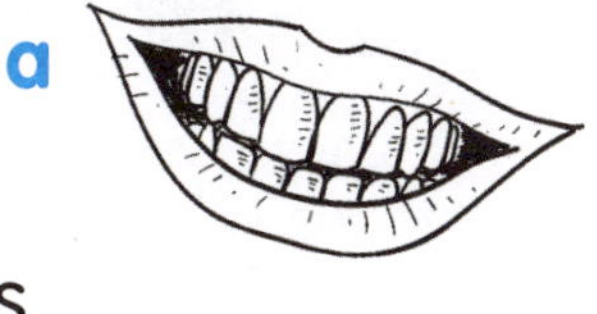
s ______

b 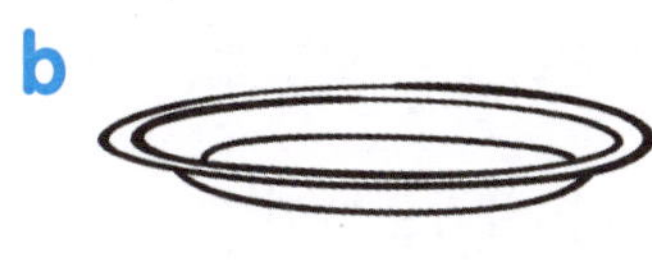
p ______

c 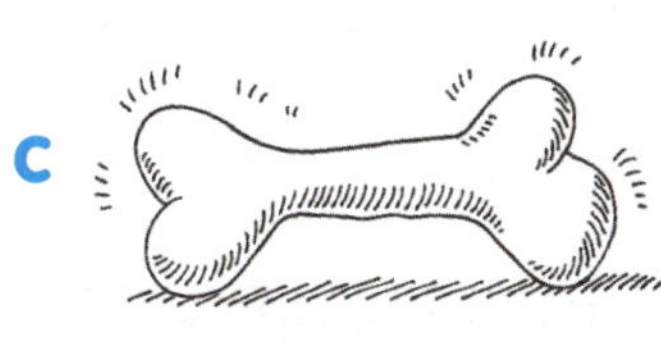
b ______

d 
n ______

3 **Write the list word that belongs in each group.**

a skeleton, skin, ______

b grin, laugh, ______

c bowl, cup, ______

d rock, pebble, ______

e knife, sword, ______

f seven, eight, ______

4 **Sort each list word into a column.**

a-e	e-e	i-e	o-e	u-e

Split digraphs

Challenge words

1 Copy each challenge word.

scrape ______	guide ______
while ______	lemonade ______
shave ______	microwave ______
tadpole ______	crocodile ______
gnome ______	
whale ______	

2 Answer the question with a challenge word.

a What reptile has large snapping jaws with lots of sharp teeth? ______

b What delicious drink can you make with lemons, sugar and water? ______

c What is a young frog called? ______

d What animal lives underwater and breathes through its blowhole? ______

e What can you use to heat up food? ______

3 Complete each sentence with a challenge word.

a I had to ______ the melted cheese off the pan.

b Dad uses a razor and soap to ______ his face.

c The ______ had started to grow long legs.

d Grandma bought a new ______ for her garden.

Prepositions

Prepositions are important words that come before **nouns** and **pronouns**. They help to tell **where**, **when** or **how**; e.g., **in** the house, **at** midday, **with** a spoon.

1 Circle the correct preposition.

a We are going (to, for) the library.

b He looked (on, out) the window.

c They walked (past, up) the museum.

d I sat (from, beside) my friend on the bus.

e I cleaned it (above, with) soap and water.

f I bought my mother a box (to, of) chocolates.

g I heard a scream (on, in) the middle of the night.

2 Complete each sentence with a preposition from the box. Use each preposition once.

past	on
above	at
for	in
under	

a I waited ________________ the train station.

b We drove ________________ an amusement park.

c The clouds float ________________ the earth.

d My friend's party is ________________ Saturday.

e My cat was hiding ________________ my bed.

f We haven't seen them ________________ a long time.

g She blew out the candles ________________ a single breath.

3 Use the picture to help you complete the sentences.

The pirate has a red hat ____________ his head. There is a sword ____________ his belt. He has boots ____________ his feet.

Haikus

Visualisation

Good readers imagine pictures when they read. They use their senses to help them visualise.

Haiku poems show a moment in time. They have few words and readers fill in the gaps by visualising.

Read the passage.

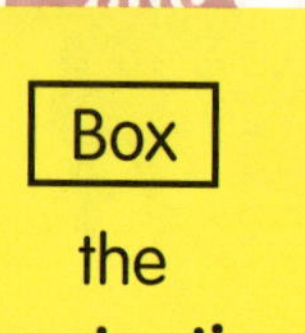

Circle **what** is in the room.

Box the **punctuation marks**.

Underline the **adjectives**.

Colour the **repeated** phrase.

A man, just one—
also a fly, just one—
in the huge drawing room

Kobayashi Issa

Circle the correct answers.

1. Which **two** things are in the drawing room?
   - a man
   - b huge
   - c bay
   - d fly
2. Which **two** punctuation marks are used?
   - a question marks
   - b commas
   - c colons
   - d dashes
3. **What** do these punctuation marks tell the reader to do?
   - a shout
   - b pause
   - c whisper
   - d look up
4. Which word **best** describes how the drawing room would look?
   - a crowded
   - b empty
   - c full
   - d noisy

Haikus

Box the word that describes the **feel** of the egg.

Warm snug speckled egg
Dappled light fading quickly
Soft crack of split shell

Alysha Hodge

Underline words that describe what the egg **looks like**.

Colour words that describe the **light**.

Circle the correct answer.

1. At what **time of day** is the poet looking at the egg?

   a morning b late at night c midday d late afternoon

2. Which phrase describes the **sound** of the egg breaking?

   a dappled b warm snug c fading quickly d soft crack

3. To hear this sound, how far away is the poet from the egg?

   a far away b behind it in a field
   c very close d in the next town

4. What is the poet **seeing**?

   a a person taking a photo of an egg
   b two chickens wrapped in a warm blanket
   c two farmers ploughing the field
   d a bird hatching

Digraphs: ea, ee

Two letters that make a single sound are called a **digraph**. The **letters ea** make the **single sound ee**; e.g., team.

The **letters ee** also make the **single sound ee**; e.g., tree.

When the **digraph ee** is **separated by a consonant**, it becomes a **split digraph**; e.g., the**s**e.

1 **Copy each list word.**

meet	______	beat	______	pleat	______
meat	______	sheet	______	wheat	______
feet	______	neat	______	bleat	______
heat	______	treat	______	upbeat	______
greet	______	sweet	______	street	______
seat	______	cheat	______	repeat	______
fleet	______	tweet	______		

2 **Sort the list words.**

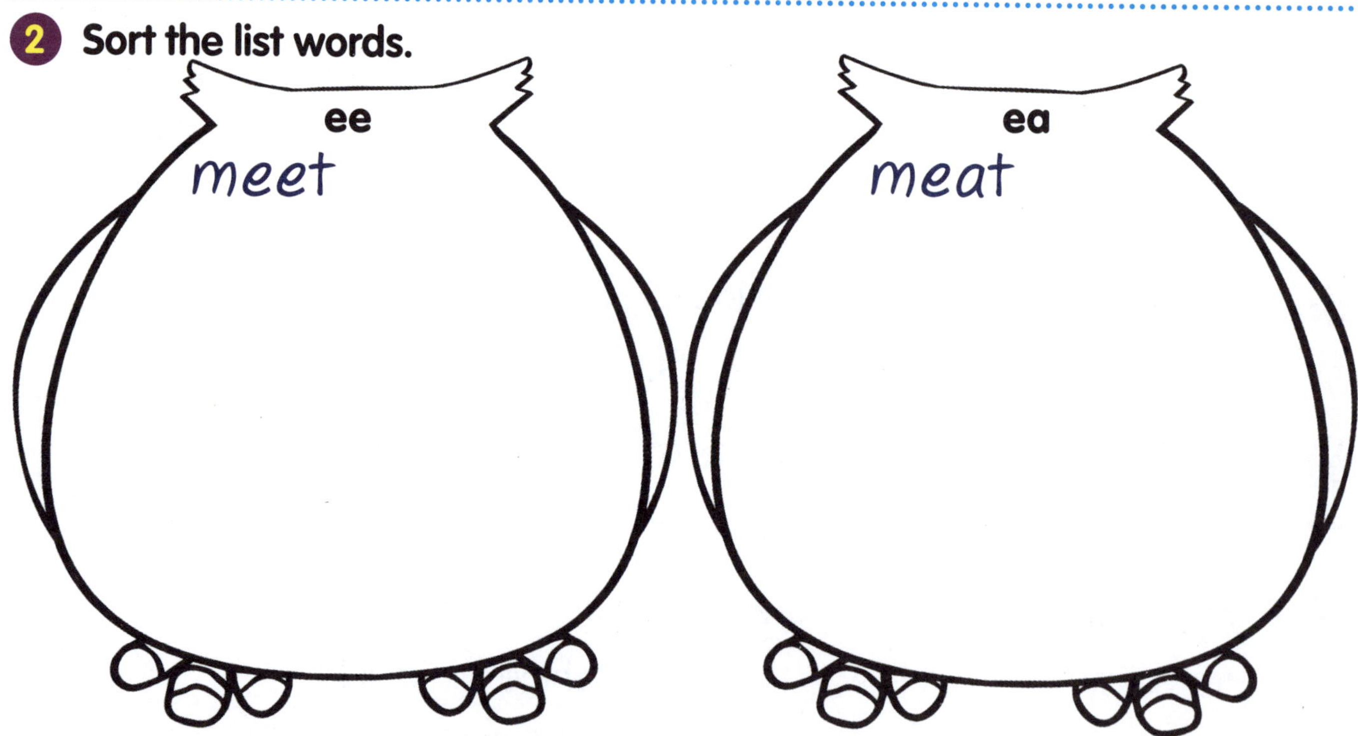

3 **Complete each sentence with a list word.**

a I opened the door to ______ our visitors.

b In summer I only need a light ______ on my bed.

c I couldn't find my shoes, so I ran to the shops in bare ______.

d My friend and I live on the same ______.

Digraphs: ea, ee

1 Which list word means?

a a group of ships ______

b the sound made by a goat or sheep ______

c to defeat a person ______

d the sound made by a bird ______

e a grain used to make flour ______

Challenge words

2 Copy each challenge word.

compete	______	parakeet	______
delete	______	retreat	______
defeat	______	complete	______
overeat	______	concrete	______
athlete	______	heartbeat	______

3 Which challenge word means?

a to eat too much ______

b to move back or away from something ______

c someone who participates in sports ______

d a small, brightly coloured parrot ______

4 Colour the correct word.

a I decided not to compete / compet in this year's fun run.

b I ran a complet / complete circuit of the oval.

c The doctor listened to my heartbeat / heartbeet.

Adverb groups

Adverb groups tell us **where**, **when** or **how**; e.g., **in** the ocean, **at** midnight, **with** a smile, **into** quarters.

1 Complete each sentence with a word from the box.

since
in
against
with

a The boy was leaning ________________ the wall.

b The pie is baking ____________ the oven.

c I haven't eaten ________________ this morning.

d She washed her hands ________________ special soap.

2 Does the underlined phrase tell where, when or how?

a The party starts **at two o'clock**. ______________

b The baby dropped the spoon **on the floor**. ______________

c I wiped up the mess **with an old cloth**. ______________

d The movie starts **in an hour's time**. ______________

e She cut the ribbon **into two halves**. ______________

3 Complete the phrase.

a I left my hat ____________ home.

b We travelled to Perth ____________ plane.

c Tomorrow I have to go ____________ the dentist.

d They delivered our furniture ____________ the morning.

Week 31 Day 1 Comprehension

The Fox and the Grapes

Finding the main idea

The main idea of a text is its key point. It sums up what the text is about. Details in the text can help you find the main idea.

Read the passage.

words that describe the **fox**.

Colour the fox's **dialogue**.

A hungry fox was looking for food. She saw bunches of juicy, plump grapes growing high up on a farmer's fence.

"I will have those grapes. I'm starving!" she said.

Underline words that describe the **grapes**.

Circle the correct answer/s.

1. Which **best** describes the main idea of the text?
   - a A fox wanted to become a farmer.
   - b A farmer was growing juicy, plump grapes.
   - c A greedy farmer put food too high for the fox.
   - d A hungry fox was looking for food.

2. Which **two** text details **support** the main idea?
   - a growing high up
   - b hungry fox
   - c plump grapes
   - d I'm starving!

3. Which **best** describes what the fox plans to do?
   - a Steal the fence.
   - b Eat the grapes.
   - c Starve the farmer.
   - d Grow grapes.

The Fox and the Grapes

Read the passage.

The fox ran at the fence and leapt as high as she could. It was a great leap—but it wasn't high enough. She hadn't even reached the lowest bunch of grapes.

The fox tried again. She ran and leapt and it was another wonderful leap. But once again, she did not jump high enough to reach the fruit. She didn't give up though.

Circle **two verbs** that tell how the fox moved.

Underline **adjectives** that describe the leaps.

Box **what** the fox was trying to reach.

1. What is the **main idea**?
   - a The fox wanted the grapes.
   - b The fox tried unsuccessfully to reach the grapes.
   - c The fox refused to give up.

2. Which **two details** helped you find the main idea?
   - a The fox leapt
   - b The fox tried

Endings: ar, er, or

Many words that end in **ar**, **er** and **or** have a similar end sound; e.g., sug**ar**, butt**er**, doct**or**.

1 Copy each list word.

sugar ______	gather ______	cracker ______
butter ______	number ______	saucer ______
doctor ______	pepper ______	wander ______
finger ______	dollar ______	tractor ______
enter ______	brother ______	together ______
dinner ______	mirror ______	another ______
spider ______	sister ______	

2 Name.

a t ______

b s ______

c d ______

d s ______

3 Write the list word that belongs in each group.

a lunch, breakfast, ______

b wafer, cookie, ______

c sister, mother, ______

d plate, dish, ______

e hand, palm, ______

f field, crops, ______

4 Unscramble the letters to make a list word.

a teren ______

b thertoge ______

c rormir ______

d therano ______

e derwan ______

f perpep ______

Endings: ar, er, or

1 Underline the spelling mistake. Write the word correctly.

a The docter gave Isha some medicine. ____________

b Michael set the salt and peppor on the table. ____________

c I found a doller in the pocket of my jeans. ____________

d I found him looking at his reflection in the mirrar. ____________

e We were told not to wandor off without mum. ____________

Challenge words

2 Copy each challenge word.

answer ____________	October ____________
feather ____________	November ____________
deliver ____________	cellar ____________
lawyer ____________	alligator ____________
September ____________	caterpillar ____________

3 Read the clue. Complete the sentence with a challenge word.

a I look like a crocodile. I am an ____________.

b August is before me and October is after me. I am ____________.

c I am the second last month of the year. I am ____________.

d I am found on birds. I am a ____________.

4 Use as many list words as possible to make a silly story.

____

____

____

Simple sentences

A **sentence** is a group of words that makes complete sense; e.g., **I am eating breakfast**.

A simple sentence has one **subject** (the person or thing doing the action) and one **verb** (the action); e.g., **The boy** (subject) **is helping** (verb) his friend.

1 [✔] the sentences.

a [ ] The children are playing baseball.

b [ ] in the house near the beach

c [ ] past the castle and up the hill

d [ ] I am walking towards the castle.

e [ ] There's a lamp next to my bed.

2 Add extra information to each sentence.

I wore my new costume *to the party*.

a She dropped the ball ____________________.

b Noah read the story ____________________.

c Marie drew a picture ____________________.

d They wrote their names ____________________.

3 Write each sentence as a question.

I have read that book. *Have you read that book?*

a They are having lunch.

Are ______________________________.

b The monkey is swinging in the tree.

Is ______________________________.

Wet

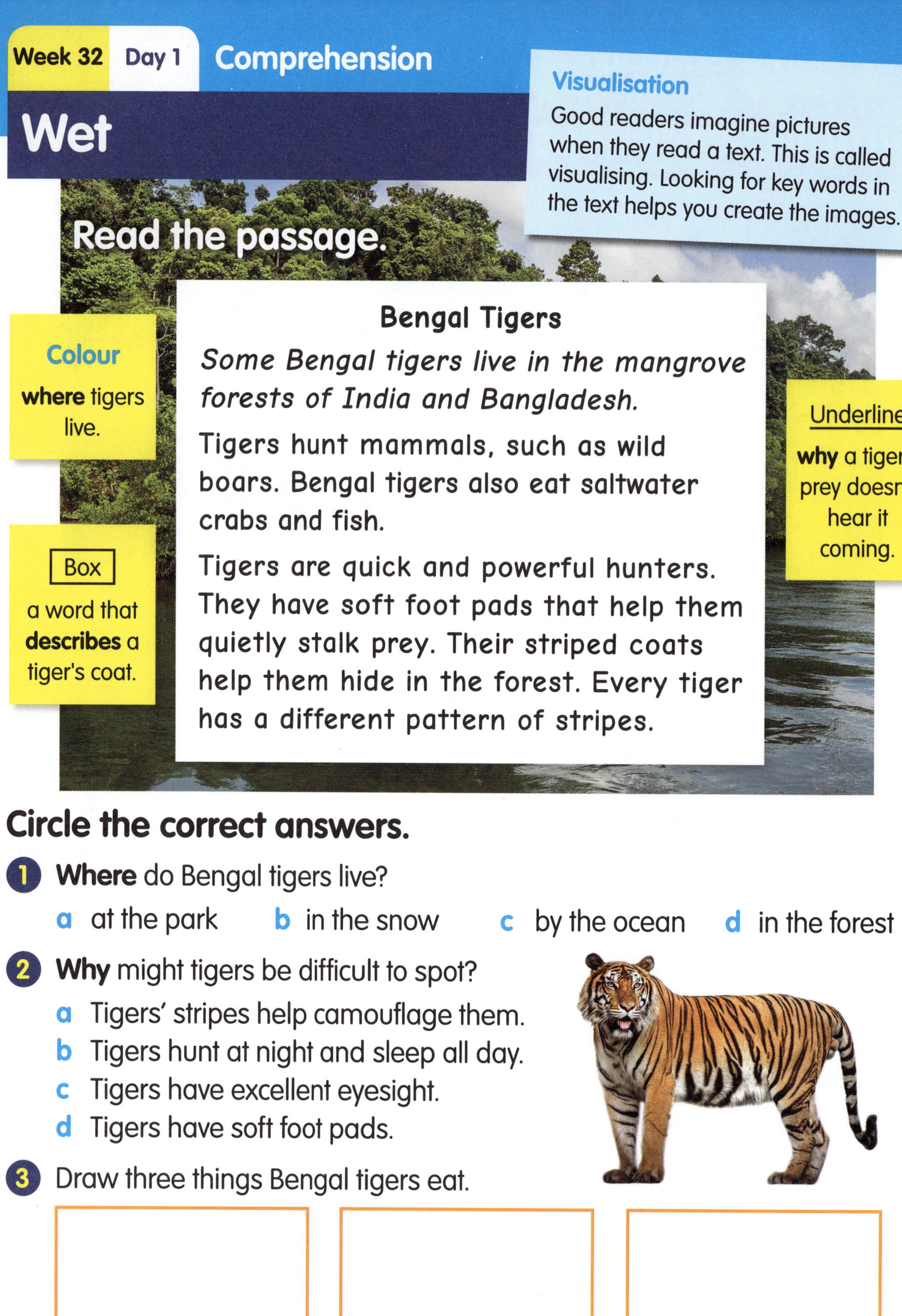

Visualisation

Good readers imagine pictures when they read a text. This is called visualising. Looking for key words in the text helps you create the images.

Read the passage.

Colour **where** tigers live.

Box a word that **describes** a tiger's coat.

Underline **why** a tiger's prey doesn't hear it coming.

Bengal Tigers

Some Bengal tigers live in the mangrove forests of India and Bangladesh.

Tigers hunt mammals, such as wild boars. Bengal tigers also eat saltwater crabs and fish.

Tigers are quick and powerful hunters. They have soft foot pads that help them quietly stalk prey. Their striped coats help them hide in the forest. Every tiger has a different pattern of stripes.

Circle the correct answers.

1 **Where** do Bengal tigers live?

a at the park b in the snow c by the ocean d in the forest

2 **Why** might tigers be difficult to spot?

a Tigers' stripes help camouflage them.
b Tigers hunt at night and sleep all day.
c Tigers have excellent eyesight.
d Tigers have soft foot pads.

3 Draw three things Bengal tigers eat.

Wet

Read the full text

Read the passage.

Colour **where** hippos live.

Box **how** a hippo moves.

Underline **what** is on top of a hippo's head.

Hippopotamuses

Hippos live in swampy lakes and rivers in Africa.

Hippos spend the day in the water. A hippo's eyes, ears and nostrils are on the top of its head. It can watch for danger while the rest of its body is underwater.

Hippos nurse their young and even sleep underwater. Hippos do not truly swim. They run or walk along the river bed.

Hippos are often aggressive. They open their mouths to warn off intruders.

1. Draw and label a picture of a hippo based on information in this text. You can make connections to hippos you've read about in stories, seen on safari or at the zoo.

Week 32 Day 3 Spelling

Digraphs: ai, a-e

Two letters that make a single sound are called a **digraph**. The **letters ai** make the **single sound ay**; e.g., pa**i**d.

When the **digraph ae** is **separated by a consonant**, it becomes a **split digraph**; e.g., lemon**ade**.

1 Copy each list word.

parade ______	grade ______	upgrade ______
paid ______	blade ______	afraid ______
made ______	raid ______	decade ______
wade ______	aid ______	invade ______
maid ______	trade ______	arcade ______
laid ______	shade ______	sunshade ______
fade ______	spade ______	

2 Which list word means?

a someone who is paid to do housework ______

b ten years ______

c a tool used for digging ______

d to give help to someone in need ______

e a sudden surprise attack ______

3 Complete the list words.

a in _ _ d _ b b _ _ de c wad _

d sunsh _ _ _ e tra _ _ f ar _ _ d _

4 Write the list words in alphabetical order.

______ ______ ______ ______

______ ______ ______ ______

______ ______ ______ ______

______ ______ ______ ______

______ ______ ______ ______

Digraphs: ai, a-e

Challenge words

1 Copy each challenge word.

cascade ____________

braid ____________

unafraid ____________

grenade ____________

mermaid ____________

lemonade ____________

bridesmaid ____________

persuade ____________

repaid ____________

marmalade ____________

2 Colour the correct word.

a I plaited her long hair into a braid breid.

b Tim spread marmelaid marmalade on his toast.

c My sister will be a bridesmeid bridesmaid at our cousin's wedding.

d I poured everyone a cool glass of lemonaid lemonade.

e Cherry tried to persuade persuad her mother to buy ice cream.

3 Which challenge word means?

a a small waterfall ____________

b a small bomb thrown by hand ____________

c talk someone into ____________

Punctuate simple sentences

A **sentence** starts with a **capital letter**. It ends with a **full stop**, **question mark** or **exclamation mark**; e.g., **T**he book is on the shelf**.** **W**here is the book**?** **W**hat a great book that was**!**

1 Fill in the missing end punctuation.

a My favourite colour is blue

b Which bike is yours

c What a crazy idea

d An octopus has eight tentacles

e Where do you live

2 [✔] the sentences that have the correct punctuation.

a [ ] He is putting on his shoes.

b [ ] where are my red socks.

c [ ] What a great time we had!

d [ ] I have lost my gloves?

e [ ] When does it start?

3 Write each sentence using the correct punctuation.

a i have a dog and a cat

____

____

b how old are you today

____

____

Farms

Compare and contrast

When you compare and contrast information, you look for **similarities** and **differences**.

Read the passage.

Vegetables

Many vegetables need a certain temperature to grow well. Some vegetables that grow well in cooler weather are carrots, onions and winter lettuce. Tomatoes, corn and capsicums need hot, sunny weather to grow well.

Some vegetables, such as lettuce and capsicums, are quick growing. Lettuce is ready to eat in six to eight weeks. Other vegetables, such as carrots, tomatoes, onions and corn take four to five months to grow and ripen.

1 Complete the table using ticks [✔].

Vegetable	Grows best in cooler weather	Grows best in warmer weather	Quick to grow	Longer to grow
carrot				
corn				
capsicum				
onion				
winter lettuce				
tomato				

2 Put a [✔] next to true information.

a ☐ Carrots and corn are quick-growing vegetables.

b ☐ Onions and tomatoes are best to grow in winter.

c ☐ Capsicums are quick-growing vegetables that like warm weather.

d ☐ You would have more tomatoes and corn in summer than in winter.

e ☐ Winter lettuce likes cool weather.

Farms

Read the full text

Farms

Read the passage.

Cows and Sheep

Some farmers raise large herds of cattle. Others raise large flocks of sheep.

Farmers raise herds of cows, called cattle, for their meat and hides. Leather is made into shoes, clothes and furniture. Cattle eat grass in fields or are fed hay and grain.

Dairy cows make milk. Milk can be made into cheese, yoghurt and ice cream.

Farmers raise sheep for their wool, meat and milk. Farmers shear sheep once a year. The wool can be made into jumpers, blankets and carpets.

Box what farmers use **cows** for.

Underline the name for a **group of cows**.

Colour what farmers use **sheep** for.

Circle the name for a **group of sheep**.

1 Use the information in the text to compare and contrast sheep and cattle.

Sheep

Sheep and Cattle

Cattle

Week 33 Day 3 Spelling

Word building

New words are formed by adding **prefixes**; e.g., **un**happy, or **suffixes**; e.g., try, try**ing**, tri**ed**.

1 Copy each list word.

law	____________	fright	____________
lawful	____________	frighten	____________
unlawful	____________	frightened	____________
try	____________	happily	____________
trying	____________	happiness	____________
tried	____________	happiest	____________
watch	____________	begin	____________
watching	____________	beginning	____________
watched	____________	beginner	____________
watchful	____________	began	____________

2 Add suffixes to build words.

	happy	watch	begin
a			
b			
c			

3 Complete each sentence with a list word.

a The thief was arrested for breaking the ____________.

b It is ____________ to steal from other people.

c The loud thunder gave me a ____________.

d I am ____________ of large spiders.

e My brother is ____________ cartoons in the lounge room.

Word building

1 Unscramble the letters to make a list word.

a chedwat ____________ b chfulwat ____________

c inesshapp ____________ d inningbeg ____________

e innerbeg ____________ f ghtfri ____________

Challenge words

2 Copy each challenge word.

garden ____________ decision ____________

gardening ____________ friend ____________

gardener ____________ friendly ____________

decide ____________ friendliness ____________

deciding ____________ unfriendly ____________

3 Complete each sentence with a challenge word.

a Lin is helping plant vegetables in the community ____________.

b Shay and Mat are still ____________ which movie to see.

c The ____________ was not happy with the state of her roses.

d Our new neighbour did not seem to be very ____________.

e I couldn't ____________ which book I liked better.

4 Use as many challenge words as possible to make a silly story.

____

____

____

Compound sentences

A **compound sentence** has two or more simple sentences joined with the conjunctions, **and**, **but** or **so**; e.g., Ella drew. James painted. Ella drew **and** James painted.

1 Complete each sentence with a conjunction from the box.

and	or
but	so

a They got in the car __________ they drove off.

b It was getting dark __________ I went inside.

c Jack's birthday is in May __________ Gina's is in June.

d We can go to the movies __________ we can go to the beach.

e I looked in my room __________ my kitten wasn't there.

2 Colour the conjunction and underline the verbs.

a Jemma fed the dogs and Miles bathed them.

b Amelia packed her bag but she left it at home.

c It was very hot so I stayed indoors.

d Drink the juice immediately or put it in the fridge.

3 Join the two sentences with the conjunction.

a Max plays basketball. Abby plays baseball. (and)

____

____

b Jackson is tall. Joshua is taller. (but)

____

____

Week 34 Day 1 Comprehension

Fighter Planes

Sequencing events
To identify the sequence of events in a text, look at words that give clues to the order in which things happen.

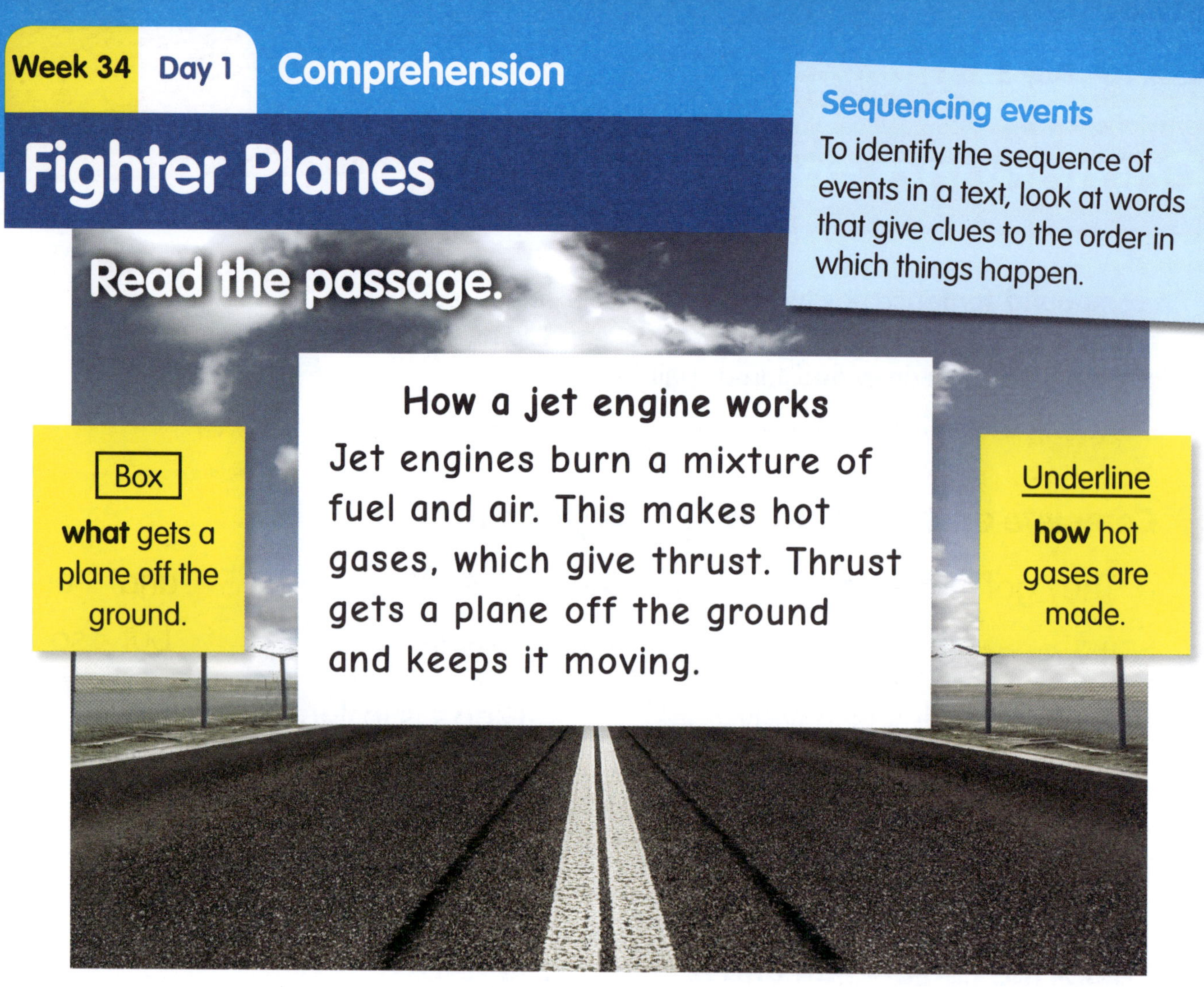

1. What does a jet engine burn?
   - a thrust and ground
   - b fuel and air
   - c gases and thrust
   - d jets and air

2. Order the events using the numbers 1–5.
   - ☐ The hot gases give thrust.
   - ☐ Thrust lifts a plane off the ground
   - ☐ Jet engines burn a mixture of fuel and air.
   - ☐ Thrust keeps the fighter plane moving.
   - ☐ The mix of fuel and air makes hot gases.

Fighter Planes

Read the full text

Read the passage.

Colour **what** helps a plane get off the ground.

Swing Wings

Wide wings help get a plane off the ground. They also slow it down in the sky. Swing wings solve this problem. On fighters like the F-14 Tomcat, the wings sweep back once the jet is in the air.

Underline a **type** of fighter plane.

1. **What** helps a plane take off?

2. On an F-14 Tomcat, **where** are the wings at take-off?

3. On an F-14 Tomcat, **when** do the wings sweep back?

4. **What** do you predict will happen to the wings when it is time to land?

Week 34 Day 3 Spelling

Suffixes: er, est

Add the **suffixes er** or **est** to adjectives that compare two or more items. If the adjective **ends in a consonant** after a short vowel, **double the consonant** before adding **er** or **est**; e.g., big → bi**gg**er → bi**gg**est.

If the adjective **ends in y**, change the **y to i** before adding **er** or **est**; e.g., smelly → smell**ier** → smell**iest**.

1 Copy each list word.

bigger	happier
biggest	happiest
fattest	healthier
tinier	healthiest
tiniest	angrier
easier	angriest
easiest	flatter
saddest	busiest
heavier	funnier
heaviest	funniest

2 Sort the list words.

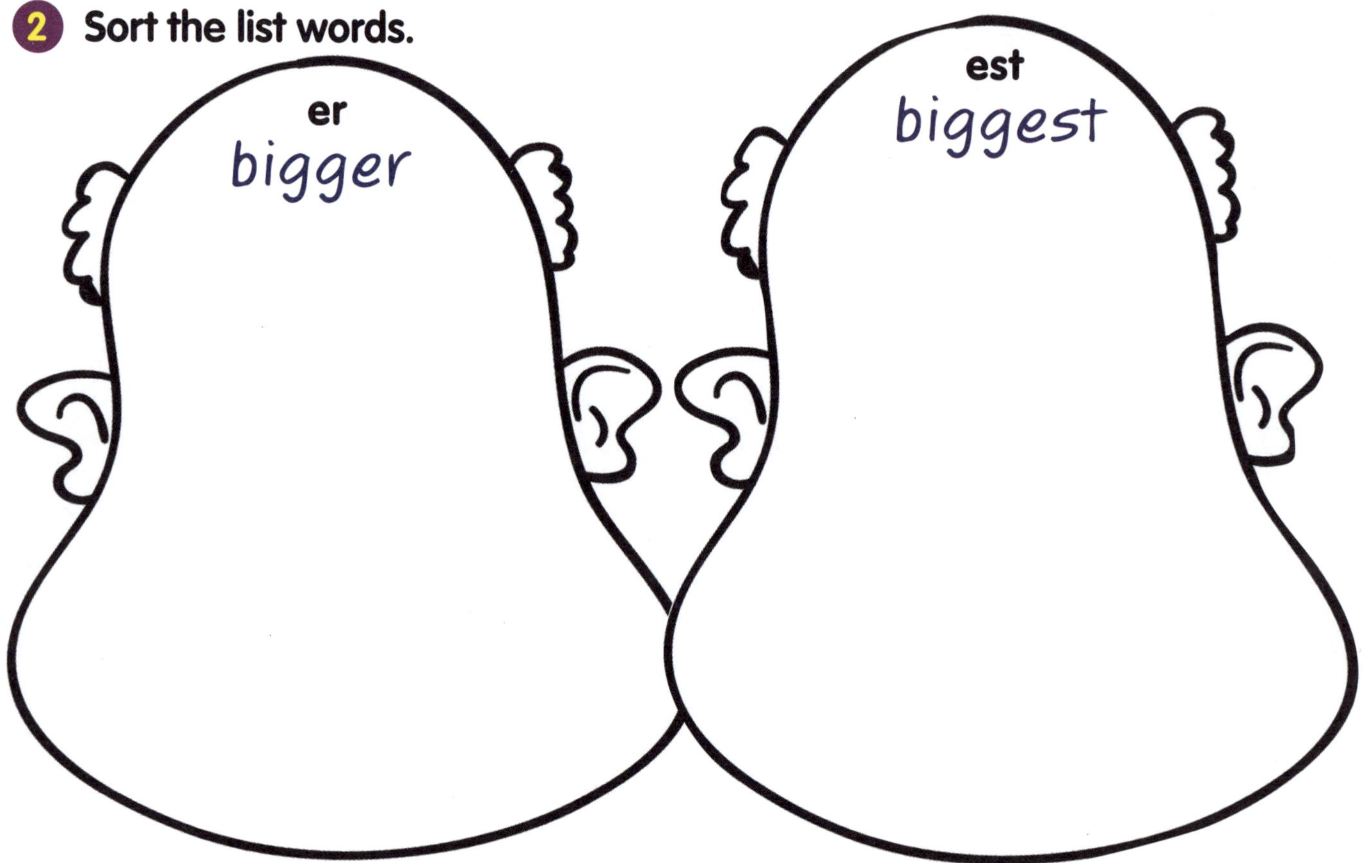

Suffixes: er, est

1 Complete each sentence with a list word.

a The elephant is ________________ than the zebra.

b That was the ________________ joke I have ever heard.

c The blue whale is the ________________ animal in the world.

d That was the ________________ karate competition we've done this year.

e I am ________________ when I am with my friends.

Challenge words

2 Copy each challenge word.

dirtiest	________________	smelliest	________________
tidier	________________	thinnest	________________
fittest	________________	scariest	________________
dimmer	________________	fluffier	________________
dirtier	________________	curliest	________________

3 Complete each sentence with a challenge word.

a The orange kitten's fur is ________________ than the black kitten's fur.

b This light bulb is ________________ than that one.

c Her hair is by far the ________________ I have ever seen!

d Mark's room is ________________ than mine.

4 Colour the correct word.

a I found the smelliest smeliest sock in my brother's swim bag.

b She made me watch the scarist scariest movie!

c I snapped the thinnest thinest branch.

Capitalising proper nouns

The names of particular **places**, **holidays** and **products** are **proper nouns**; e.g., **A**ustralia, **H**alloween, **M**icrosoft. All of the words in a proper noun start with a capital letter; e.g., **S**ydney, **G**reat **B**arrier **R**eef.

1 Circle the word that needs a capital letter.

a river murray

b everest mountain

c holiday christmas

d smartphone apple

e city melbourne

f australia country

2 Colour the words that need a capital letter.

a uluru is in the northern territory.

b We have two cars—a ford and a toyota.

c My cousin goes to ravenscliff primary school.

d Many people wear green on saint patrick's day.

e I have never been to europe, africa or south america.

3 Write this sentence with the correct capitalisation.

My best friend lives in simpson street.

____

____

Healthy Eating

Compare and contrast

To compare and contrast information, look for the **similarities** and **differences** between details in the text.

Read the passage.

Underline **what** is in a balanced diet.

Circle different **types** of dairy foods.

Colour **why** we need good food.

Healthy Foods

Your body needs a variety of good foods to grow and stay healthy.

The food we eat is called our diet. A balanced diet contains a wide variety of foods.

Carbohydrates in foods such as bread and rice give us energy. Other foods, like fruits and vegetables, are full of vitamins and minerals.

We need protein to make muscles, skin and hair. Meat and eggs are high-protein foods. We need calcium for our teeth and bones. Dairy foods, like cheese and milk, are high in calcium.

1 Complete the table.

	Why we need them	Examples
Carbohydrates		
Fruit and vegetables		
Protein		
Dairy		

Healthy Eating

Read the full text

Read the passage.

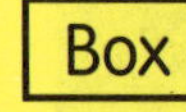
Box **what** can be made with grains.

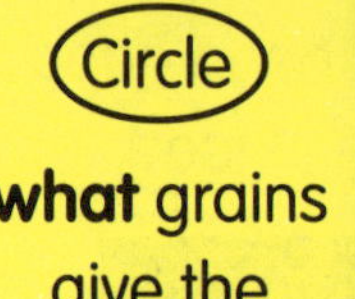
Circle **what** grains give the body.

Grains

A healthy diet should include grains, such as wheat, rice and corn.

Some grain is cooked and eaten whole. These are wholegrain foods. Other grain is ground into flour to make bread, pasta and cereals. All grains have carbohydrates, which give the body energy.

Some wholegrain foods are corn on the cob, rice and wholegrain bread. They are high in fibre. Wholegrains contain magnesium, a mineral that helps build strong bones and teeth.

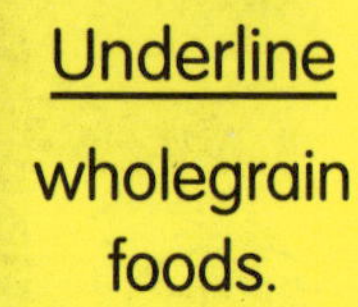
Underline wholegrain foods.

1. What do all grains give the body?

   ____

2. What extra nutrients do wholegrains give the body?

   ____

   ____

3. What is magnesium good for?

   ____

   ____

Tricky words

Some words are trickier to spell than others. Not all words follow the rules. Some have letters that are not supposed to be there. Some leave out letters. Some have letters in the wrong order.

1 Copy each list word.

I	______	with	______	pretty	______
again	______	there	______	who	______
always	______	off	______	mother	______
next	______	here	______	father	______
have	______	around	______	outside	______
were	______	wanted	______	when	______
things	______	school	______		

2 Which list word means?

a a place for teaching and learning ______

b any space that is not inside ______

c a female parent ______

d a male parent ______

3 Write the opposite.

a on ______ b unwanted ______

c ugly ______ d without ______

e inside ______ f never ______

4 Complete each sentence with a list word.

a Our neighbours ______ a huge trampoline.

b I took ______ my shoes before entering the house.

c We spun ______ in circles.

d We need to get off at the ______ bus stop.

Tricky words

1 Underline the spelling mistake. Write the word correctly.

a Ie am seven years old. ____________

b Mum told us to play outsde in the garden. ____________

c I wantid a new computer but I got a book instead. ____________

d I went to the zoo weth my grandma and grandpa. ____________

e I got it wrong so I had to start all over agein. ____________

Challenge words

2 Copy each challenge word.

every	____________	children	____________
once	____________	people	____________
happening	____________	swimming	____________
scared	____________	women	____________
favourite	____________	February	____________

3 Complete each sentence with a challenge word.

a The ____________ were excited to play in the snow.

b On hot days we like to go ____________ in the pool.

c My birthday is in ____________, the second month of the year.

d Chocolate is my ____________ flavour of ice cream.

e I am ____________ of big hairy spiders.

4 Use as many challenge words as possible to make a silly sentence.

____

____

Expanding sentences

You can use **because**, **while** or **if** to add extra information to sentences; e.g,

I liked the book **because** it was funny.

We ate lunch **while** we watched the seal show.

Henry said we could go **if** I put on a coat.

1 Use *because* to expand these sentences.

a I liked the film ______________________________

______________________________.

b I'm going to the beach ______________________________

______________________________.

c We're running for the ferry ______________________________

______________________________.

2 Use *because, while* or *if* to complete the sentences.

a I played quietly ______________ Dad talked to Dr Nisha.

b Please wash your hands ______________ we're going to eat now.

c Ally will swim ______________ it's a warm day.

d I often get distracted ______________ I'm reading in the garden.

e I don't like watermelon ______________ it's too sweet.

f We played card games ______________ we waited to board the flight.

g Dad swept the kitchen ______________ Eli washed up.

Clothes

Making inferences

Use **clues** in the text to make inferences. The clues will help you find the answers that are hiding in the text.

Read the passage.

when machinery for making clothes was invented.

Box **the adjective** that describes clothes of the 1800s.

Underline **the invention** that led to clothes being mass-produced.

1800s

During the 1800s, machinery for making clothes was invented. More factories were built. Textiles became mass-produced.

Before machinery, weavers and tailors made clothes by hand.

Sewing machines were invented and then mass-produced during the 1800s. This allowed women at home to make clothing quickly and easily. Clothes of the 1800s were often uncomfortable to wear. Women wore bone corsets that laced up tightly.

Circle the correct answer/s.

1. Which **best** describes the big change in the clothing industry in the 1800s?
   - a Machinery was used to make clothes.
   - b Sewing machines were affordable but uncomfortable.
   - c Women liked to make fashionable clothing.
   - d Men made clothes.

2. Which **clues** tell you this?
   - a Women wore bone corsets that laced up tightly.
   - b During the 1800s, machinery for making clothes was invented.
   - c More factories were built.
   - d Clothes of the 1800s were often uncomfortable to wear.
   - e Sewing machines were invented and then mass-produced during the 1800s.
   - f This allowed women at home to make clothing quickly and easily.

Clothes

Read the passage.

Underline popular clothes in the 1990s.

Box the description of **swimming costumes**.

1990s

During the 1990s, people wore shirts, hats and sunglasses to protect against skin cancer.

Hats were not popular in the 1970s and 1980s. In the 1990s, people became more aware of skin cancer. Hats became common again.

Many swimming costumes, especially for young children, once again covered much of the body. This was to protect them from the sun.

1. Draw people dressed for the beach in the 1970s and 1990s.

1970s	1990s

Week 36 Day 3 Spelling

Suffixes: ment, ness

Adding the **suffix ment** to a verb turns it into a noun; e.g., enjoy**ment**. Adding the **suffix ness** to an adjective turns it into a noun; e.g., weak**ness**.

1 Copy each list word.

illness	______	laziness	______
payment	______	fairness	______
sadness	______	enjoyment	______
darkness	______	thickness	______
fitness	______	blackness	______
sickness	______	amusement	______
richness	______	movement	______
neatness	______	statement	______
weakness	______	amazement	______
softness	______	treatment	______

2 Complete the list word.

a fit _ _ _ _ b enjoy _ _ _ _ c soft _ _ _ _

d thick _ _ _ _ e black _ _ _ _ f dark _ _ _ _

3 Unscramble these list words.

a ntmepay ______ b ntmeeattr ______

c nessfair ______ d momevent ______

e ntmemusea ______ f menteamaz ______

4 Underline the spelling mistake. Write the word correctly.

a I felt sadnes when my friend moved away. ______

b I turned on a light to see in the darknes. ______

c The crowd looked on in amazment. ______

Suffixes: ment, ness

Challenge words

1 Copy each challenge word.

argument	______	punishment	______
excitement	______	astonishment	______
gentleness	______	equipment	______
willingness	______	tiredness	______
entertainment	______	enchantment	______

2 Complete each sentence with a challenge word.

a My brother and I always have an ______ about who sits in the front seat.

b Dad made us scrub the floor as ______ for our bad behaviour.

c When camping, you must remember to bring the right ______.

d Thinking about our holiday filled me with ______.

3 Colour the correct word.

a It was her [willingness] [wilngess] to learn that made her a good team player.

b We stared in [astonesment] [astonishment] at our coach's strange hat.

c They hired a clown as [entertainment] [enterteinmnt] for the party.

Formal and informal language

Informal language is usually used when speaking or writing emails to friends and family; e.g., **Hi** Jerry. Formal language is used when speaking to older people, especially if we do not know them very well; e.g., **Good morning**, Mr Clarke.

1 In each pair, colour the more informal expression.

2 In each pair, colour the more formal expression.

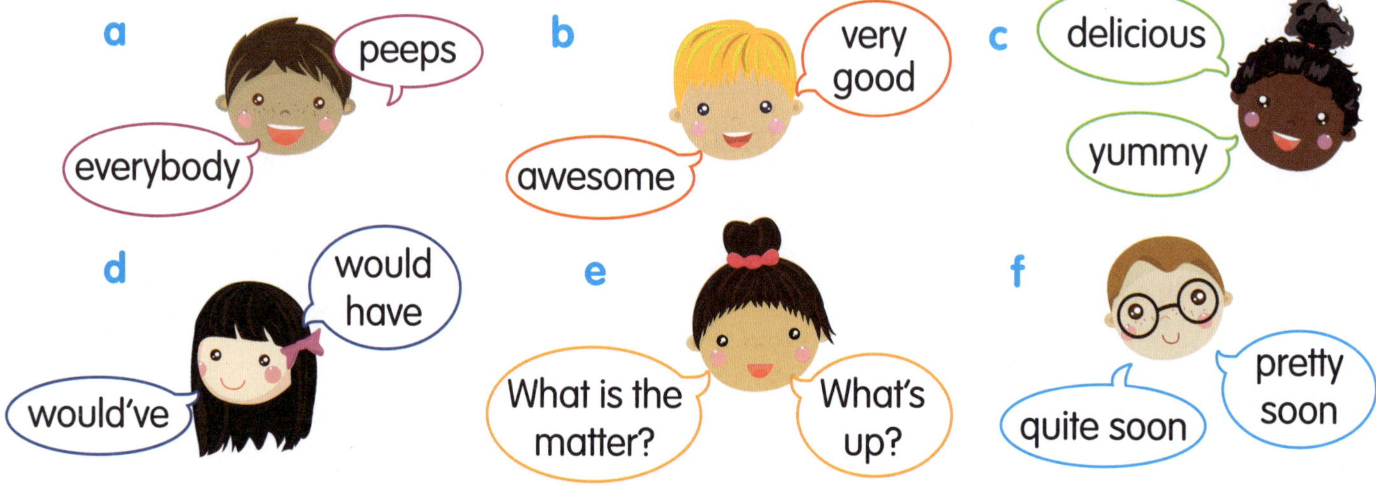

3 Rewrite the sentence so that it sounds more formal.

You wanna come with me? *Would you like to come with me?*

I haven't ever been to Adelaide.

____

____

Spelling

Use this review to test your knowledge. It has three parts—**Spelling**, **Grammar** and **Comprehension**. If you're unsure of an answer, go back and read the rules and generalisations in the blue boxes.

You have learned about:

- irregular past tense verbs
- endings: ar, er, or
- suffixes: er, est
- split digraphs
- digraphs: ai, a-e
- tricky words
- digraphs: ea, ee
- word building
- suffixes: ment, less

1 Complete each word with one of these. 2 marks

ai ee a-e i-e

a sk__t__ b sm__l__ c sh__ __t d afr__ __d

2 Which word completes the sentence? 1 mark

On Saturday, I ______________ to the zoo.

a go b went c goes d going

3 Add suffixes to build words with happy. 3 marks

a happy + ly = ____________________

b happy + ness = ____________________

c happy + est = ____________________

4 Complete the words with or, er or ar. 2 marks

a sauc__ __ b doll__ __ c fing__ __ d tract__ __

5 Which word completes the sentence? 1 mark

The buffalo was ______________ than the antelope.

a heaviest b heavy c heavily d heavier

6 Underline the word spelled incorrectly. Write it correctly. 1 mark

I've allways wanted to be an astronaut. ____________________

Grammar

You have learned about:

- irregular verbs
- simple sentences
- compound sentences
- formal and informal language
- prepositions
- punctuating sentences
- expanding sentences
- adverb groups
- proper nouns

1 Write the verbs in brackets in the past tense. 3 marks

a Last night I (eat) ______________ all my dinner.

b This morning I (drink) ______________ a glass of milk.

c Last week Simon (bring) ______________ his dog to basketball practice.

2 Circle the correct preposition. 2 marks

a The toy was spinning (around, on) the room.

b I dipped my toes (in, over) the water.

3 Complete the phrase with a preposition. 2 marks

a The librarian greeted us ______________ a smile.

b Birds build their nests ______________ trees.

4 In each sentence, circle the verb. 2 marks

a The cow sat quietly under a tree.

b The dogs dug holes in the garden.

Grammar

5 Write each sentence with the correct punctuation. 2 marks

a she has lost her keys ______________________________

____

b what are they doing ______________________________

____

6 Expand each sentence. 4 marks

a Amy likes football because ______________________________

______________________________.

b Kate practised the flute while ______________________________

______________________________.

7 Join the two sentences with the conjunction. 1 mark

Becky has a white cat. Lucy has a black cat. (and)

____

____

8 Colour the words that need a capital letter. 2 marks

a We celebrated anzac day in hobart.

b We took the ferry from circular quay to manly.

9 In each pair, colour the more formal expression. 2 marks

a Hi | Good morning

b How R U? | How are you?

Your score ___ / 20

How Can We Attract Birds into Our Gardens?

Read the passage and then use the comprehension skills you have learned to answer the questions.

According to Professor Scott, one way we shouldn't be attracting birds into our gardens is by feeding them. The large number of birds around a bird feeder attracts cats. Also, larger birds start to take over the area while some, like crows, attack the smaller birds and eat their eggs and chicks.

Another reason for not feeding birds is that sometimes they become so used to getting food from us that they stop looking for food in the wild. In addition, the food we give them is often not the right kind and can make them ill.

Professor Scott says the best way to attract birds into our gardens is to create a wild area with native plants in it. The birds will come into the garden to feed on the pollen, seeds and fruit of these plants. They will also eat the insects in the area. In this way, they will eat their natural foods.

We should also make sure there is fresh water for the birds and we should definitely avoid using chemicals on the plants.

1 Why do people keep bird feeders in their gardens? 1 mark **LITERAL**

a to attract cats
b to attract birds
c to make sure birds don't starve
d as ornaments

2 Why would cats be attracted to birds around a bird feeder? Cats ... 1 mark **INFERENTIAL**

a prey on birds.
b play with birds.
c like to watch birds.
d steal the birds' food.

How Can We Attract Birds into Our Gardens?

3 Which of the following is a big bird? 1 mark INFERENTIAL

a a blue jay b a sparrow c a finch d a crow

4 Who is Professor Scott? Professor Scott is most likely a … 1 mark INFERENTIAL

a scientist. b farmer. c reporter. d photographer.

5 Which is a reason for not feeding birds? If we feed birds, they could … 1 mark LITERAL

a get fat. b frighten our pets.

c stop coming into our gardens. d get sick.

6 What part of a native tree do birds not eat? 1 mark INFERENTIAL

a leaves b pollen c seeds d fruit

7 Which word is the opposite of *native* in the phrase *native* plants? 1 mark VOCABULARY

a local b alien c natural d wild

8 Why does Professor Scott say we shouldn't use chemicals on plants? The chemicals might … 1 mark INFERENTIAL

a kill the plants. b improve the soil.

c get washed away by rain. d poison the birds.

9 What is the purpose of the text? 1 mark CRITICAL

a to retell an event b to give advice

c to tell a story d to explain how something works

10 Who is the target audience for this text? People who … 1 mark CRITICAL

a live in the city. b have big gardens.

c want more birds in their gardens. d have cats.

Your score ___ /10

Your Review 4 Scores

Spelling		Grammar		Comprehension		Total
/10	+	/20	+	/10	=	/40

Week 1, Day 1
Pg 2

Answers to passage will vary. Talk through responses.

1 b **2** a **3** a **4** b **5** a

Week 1, Day 2
Pg 3

A Gecko on the Teacher!

The gecko jumps onto Mr Mooney's hand. It runs up his arm. It leaps onto his head and waves at us.

Mr Mooney's eyes roll up and his mouth is the shape of an O.

His arms freeze halfway to his head, as if he's too afraid to move.

1 running up Mr Mooney's arm to his head
2 scared, afraid
3 *Answers will vary. Suggested answer:* I was surprised when my parents took me to camp in Lane Cove National Park with my cousins.

Week 1, Day 3
Pg 4

1 Check for correct spelling of each word.
2 a dancess dances **b** listenes listens **c** breakes breaks **d** buyes buys
3 a crosses **b** covers **c** melts **d** behaves **e** coaches **f** hammers
4 a melts **b** dances **c** breaks

Week 1, Day 4
Pg 5

1

break	breaks
push	pushes
bite	bites
grow	grows

2 Check for correct spelling of each word.
3 *Answers will vary. Read through the story together.*
4 a finishes **b** measures **c** vanishes **d** teaches **e** switches

Week 1, Day 5
Pg 6

1 a hat **b** sun **c** pig **d** cyclist **e** house
2 a thing **b** person **c** animal **d** place
3 a moon **b** star
4 a ant **b** doll

Week 2, Day 1
Pg 7

A Good Idea

"Haven't you ever seen a money tree?" asked Mandy.

Tim shook his head. "How do people get a money tree?"

"Easy!" Mandy laughed. "They plant a coin in a pot full of dirt. Then they water it."

"When the coin grows into a tree, flowers grow on it. The flowers turn into money," she told him.

1 a
2 b
3 c

Week 2, Day 2
Pg 8

Trouble!

Mum didn't like Mandy playing tricks on Tim.

"There's only one thing to do," Mum said. "Take the coins out of your piggybank and stick them on Tim's tree."

"But I was saving up to buy a book!" Mandy told her.

1 Mandy
2 to take the coins out of her piggybank and give them to Tim
3 she played a trick on Tim
4 a book

Week 2, Day 3
Pg 9

1 Check for correct spelling of each word.
2 a worm **b** shark **c** arm **d** storm
3 ar words: arm, warm, ward, shark, warp, spark, war, car, warn, wart, apart
or words: worm, word, storm, snort, stork, work, born, short, sport

Week 2, Day 4
Pg 10

1 a warm **b** sport **c** car **d** shark **e** wart
2 Check for correct spelling of each word.
3 *Answers will vary. Suggested answer:* to, war, dot, raw, ward, toad, row, wart, tow, road
4 a morning **b** wharf **c** corner **d** towards

Week 2, Day 5
Pg 11

1 a flock **b** pride **c** pair **d** pod **e** swarm **f** fleet
2 a litter **b** school **c** band
3 a gang/thieves **b** library/books **c** bunch/flowers

Week 3, Day 1
Pg 12

Happy Birds

Lots of cages hung in the trees. Grandpa hung Yan's cage with the others.

There were lots of grandpas and lots of songbirds. All the birds whistled. The air was full of whistles. Grandpa sat on a bench and whistled too.

Yan liked to sing with the other birds. Grandpa liked to whistle with the other grandpas.

1 d **2** c **3** a

Week 3, Day 2
Pg 13

Dear Grandpa,

The birds in Australia have bright feathers. Some are grey and pink. Others are white and wear yellow hats. They all sing very loudly.

I wish you could hear the birds, Grandpa. They are happy birds. I am sure Yan would be happy in Australia. You would be happy too.

I miss going to the park with you, Grandpa.

Love, Ling

1 Ling says they are bright, colourful and happy
2 yes: Ling says Australian birds are happy, Yan and Grandpa would be happy and that she misses going to the park with him

Week 3, Day 3
Pg 14

1 Check for correct spelling of each word.
2 a hockey **b** money **c** ninety **d** pretty **e** honey **f** turkey
3 a turkey **b** money **c** donkey **d** key
4 a mony money **b** ninty ninety **c** hocky hockey

Week 3, Day 4
Pg 15

1 any, donkey, empty, fairy, ugly
2 Check for correct spelling of each word.
3 a chimney b January c library
d parsley e family
4 a jersey b February c library
d country

Week 3, Day 5
Pg 16

1 a Check for correct name
b Check for correct month
c December
d Check for correct name
e Julia Gillard
2 Monday, Tuesday, Wednesday, Thursday, Friday, Saturday, Sunday
3 a ben Ben b bailey Bailey
c july July d brown Brown
e hilda Hilda

Week 4, Day 1
Pg 17

More Unusual Pets

A goose flew in through the window. She landed with a thump. She grumbled as she got up off the floor.

Then a hyena came to the door. He had the hiccups. He saw the goose and laughed.

They began to argue. It went on and on until Stella yelled, "Stop!"

The room was silent. The crocodile stood very still.

1 b 2 c

Week 4, Day 2
Pg 18

Rabbit Chase

"Help! Help!" yelled the rabbit. "The lion is trying to eat me!"

"I am not," said the lion. He sounded hurt. "I was trying to whisper in your ear. But one of your whiskers tickled my nose. I just slipped.

"Then your foot was in my mouth. I don't know how that happened. Mmmmmm, yummy."

1 lion/rabbit
2 a "Help! Help! The lion is trying to eat me!"
b "Mmmmmm, yummy."

Week 4, Day 3
Pg 19

1 Check for correct spelling of each word.
2 str words: street, strong, strap, strip, struck, stream, streak, stroke, strike, strain, stripe, string, stride
spr words: spray, sprint, spring
scr words: scrub, scrape, screen, scream
3 a stroke b street c strap

Week 4, Day 4
Pg 20

1 a streng string b sprent sprint
c scren screen d strype stripe
e streem stream
2 Check for correct spelling of each word.
3 a strict b stroll c screech d sprinkle
4 *Answers will vary. Read through the story together.*

Week 4, Day 5
Pg 21

1 a I b They c him d she e us
2 a me b They c you d it e She
3 a them b her c him d it

Week 5, Day 1
Pg 22

A thirsty ant came to the edge of a river to get a drink. The fast-moving water splashed the ant and knocked it into the river. The ant was in trouble! It tried to swim but it was drowning.

A dove sitting in a tree picked a leaf and dropped it in the river, near the ant. The ant climbed onto the leaf and floated to safety on the bank of the river.

1 a 2 c, d 3 b

Week 5, Day 2
Pg 23

A little while later, a hunter came to the edge of the river. He saw the dove sitting in the tree and quickly drew his bow and aimed at the resting bird. The ant saw what was about to happen. It ran over to the hunter and bit his toe as hard as it could. The hunter cried out and dropped his bow. The dove was startled and flew away to safety.

1 ant/dove
2 a bit the hunter's toe as hard as he could
b cried out and startled the dove so it could fly away

Week 5, Day 3
Pg 24

1 Check for correct spelling of each word.
2 a quake b queen c quiver
d quote e quest f quiz
3 a queen b squeak c squirrel
d quilt e quack
4 a quilt b queen c squirrel

Week 5, Day 4
Pg 25

1 Missing letters are underlined
a equal b quit c equip d quest
e quite f quaint
2 Check for correct spelling of each word.
3 a queasy b quench c question
d squelch
4 a frequent b squabble c question
d quench e squelch

Week 5, Day 5
Pg 26

1 a a b an c An/an d a/a e a/an
2 a a b a c the d an e the
f an g a
3 a an b a c an

Week 6, Day 1
Pg 27

Plants in Summer

Plants grow quickly in summer.

Many plants flower in summer. Flowers make seeds. Some flowers, like apple blossoms, become fruit. Fruit grows and ripens in the summer.

In summer, trees are covered in green leaves. The leaves make food for the tree. The trunk grows thicker.

1 a 2 b 3 c

Week 6, Day 2
Pg 28

Summer Food

We eat more fresh food in summer.

Salads are made from fresh summer vegetables. Families enjoy the outdoors by having picnics and barbeques.

Many fruits, such as berries, melons and peaches, are ripe in the summer. Fruit salad is good for you and tastes good too.

1 fresh foods
2 vegetables or fruit
3 outdoors
4 berries, melons and peaches
5 fruit salad

Week 6, Day 3
Pg 29

1 Check for correct spelling of each word.
2 ing words: saving, posing, sharing, writing, hiking, giving, wasting, gazing
ed words: closed, used, chased, changed, phoned, teased, solved, freed, raced, agreed, shaped, exploded
3 **a** closed **b** sharing **c** hiking
d posing **e** changed **f** freed

Week 6, Day 4
Pg 30

1 **a** chaased chased
b explooded exploded
c sollved solved
d agred agreed
2 Check for correct spelling of each word.
3 **a** freezing **b** created **c** arriving
4 *Answers will vary. Read through the story together.*

Week 6, Day 5
Pg 31

1 **a** the **b** my, i **c** the **d** my
e noah, i
2 **a** There is someone at the door.
b My sister can play the trumpet.
c My brother and I have our own rooms.
d Our cousins like their new house.
e Emma and I have finished our chores.
3 **a** The baby is eating his food.
b Ruby and I are sisters.

Week 7, Day 1
Pg 32

Finding Water

Water is hard to find in a dry habitat.

Birds and large mammals, such as antelopes, elephants and zebras, travel long distances to find water.

Other animals get water from the food they eat. Bilbies and kangaroo rats get water from insects, fruit, seeds and leaves.

1 ✔ a, b, e, f ✘ c, d

Week 7, Day 2
Pg 33

Conserving Water

Desert animals have special water-saving strategies.

Some animals in dry habitats do not sweat to cool down. This helps the kangaroo rat and the fennec fox to conserve water.

Reptiles have thick skins. Spiders and insects have exoskeletons. These hard, outer shells reduce water loss.

1 ✔ a, b, d, f ✘ c, e

Week 7, Day 3
Pg 34

1 Check for correct spelling of each word.
2 **a** unhappy **b** unroll **c** unable
d unkind **e** unmade **f** unwind
g untrue
3 Missing letters are underlined
a unfair **b** unlike **c** unwise
d unload **e** unsafe **f** unfit
4 **a** untrue **b** unfold **c** unhappy

Week 7, Day 4
Pg 35

1 Check for correct spelling of each word.
2 *Answers will vary. Suggested answers*: friend, friendly, end, fun, fire, nine, dine
3 **a** unlucky **b** unwrap **c** unfriendly
d unbuckle
4 **a** unhealthy **b** unhelpful **c** unusual
d untangle

Week 7, Day 5
Pg 36

1 **a** hot **b** furry **c** six **d** delicious **e** angry
2 How many? twelve, twenty, seven
What colour? blue, brown, purple
What taste? bitter, sweet, spicy
3 delicious, crispy, round, hot

Week 8, Day 1
Pg 37

Old Trains

The first trains were pulled along by steam engines.

Steam engines burn coal. The burning coal heats water to make steam. The steam makes the wheels turn.

In the 1800s steam trains were a quick and cheap way to travel for fun as well as for work. Today most steam trains are for tourists.

1 c 2 c, d

Week 8, Day 2
Pg 38

New Trains

Today, most trains have diesel or electric engines.

The new engines are quieter and cleaner than coal-powered steam engines. Diesel trains are often used in small towns. Many electric trains run in cities.

Some electric trains can travel very fast. They are called high-speed trains. The bullet trains in Japan can travel three times faster than a car.

1 new trains
2 **a** are diesel or electric.
b are quieter and cleaner than coal-powered engines.

Week 8, Day 3
Pg 39

1 Check for correct spelling of each word.
2 a tooth **b** igloo **c** foot **d** hook
3 short oo words: hook, foot, wood, took
long oo words: too, mood, room, soon, hoot, cool, tooth, broom, gloom, igloo, goose, proof, shoot, loose, groom, ooze

Week 8, Day 4
Pg 40

1 a room **b** broom **c** igloo
2 Check for correct spelling of each word.
3 a rooster **b** boomerang **c** scooter **d** poodle **e** cocoon
4 a goodbye **b** snooze **c** kangaroo

Week 8, Day 5
Pg 41

1 mice, women, people, oxen
2 a teeth **b** children **c** geese **d** feet **e** women
3 sheep, deer, moose

Week 9, Day 1
Pg 42

1 5, 4, 1, 3, 2
2 *Answers will vary. Suggested answer:* A drawing of seeds in the field with sunshine and/or rain.

Week 9, Day 2
Pg 43

Refining

Trucks carry wheat to flour mills. The wheat grains are made into flour.

People inspect the wheat to make sure it is good quality.

The grain is cleaned and soaked in water for 10 to 20 hours. This separates the outer layer of bran from the soft, inner part. Rollers crush the wheat into a powder called flour.

1 it is cleaned
2 rollers crush the wheat into a powder called flour
3 how to refine wheat

Week 9, Day 3
Pg 44

1 Check for correct spelling of each word.
2 a race **b** face **c** city **d** mice
2 Missing letters are <u>underlined</u>
a l<u>ace</u> **b** sl<u>ice</u> **c** t<u>wice</u> **d** <u>ice</u>
e O<u>nce</u> **f** n<u>ice</u>

Week 9, Day 4
Pg 45

1 a spicy **b** race **c** space **d** city **e** cell
2 Check for correct spelling of each word.
3 a juicy **b** pencil **c** prince **d** fleece **e** piece
4 a fleece **b** pencil **c** prince

Week 9, Day 5
Pg 46

1 Tick: a, d, e
2 a <u>face, feet, knees and arms</u>
b <u>monkeys, lions, hippos and zebras</u>
c <u>a circle, a triangle, a square and a rectangle</u>
d <u>a book, three pencils, a hat and a chocolate</u>
e <u>the king, the queen, the prince and the princess</u>
3 teddy bear, wand, kite, whistle

REVIEW 1
Spelling
Pg 47

1 b **2** c
3 Missing letters are <u>underlined</u>
a <u>str</u>eet **b** <u>scr</u>ub **c** <u>spr</u>int
4 a spicy **b** hockey **c** queasy **d** unhappy
5 *Answers will vary. Suggested answers*: boom, rang, room, bang, room, broom, manor, oar, game, bear, beam, bean, moon, grab

Grammar
Pg 48–49

1 a bird **b** box
2 a herd **b** pod
3 a amy **b** january
4 a she **b** her **c** they **d** them
5 a an, the **b** the, a
6 *Answers will vary. Suggested answer*: My <u>best</u> friend has <u>two</u> dogs.
7 a feet **b** men
8 a sunshine, rain and hail
b a dog, a cat, a guinea pig and a goldfish
c flour, sugar, butter and eggs
d an apple, a banana, a sandwich and a biscuit

Comprehension
Pg 50–51

1 c **2** b **3** d **4** a **5** a **6** b
7 d **8** a **9** b **10** c

Week 10, Day 1
Pg 52

Thump! Thump! Thump!

What is that?

"Thump!"

It's coming from the closet. Tim <u>creeps over</u> and slides the door open. A tiny purple alien steps out and pokes Tim on the foot.

"Take me to your weader!"

Tim jumps back on the bed. The alien is only as big as a teddy bear but he has a zap gun. The gun is pointed at Tim.

"Wha ... what?" Tim asks.

1 a **2** d **3** a

Week 10, Day 2
Pg 53

Slime Jelly

<u>"Here is some slime instead,"</u> Tim yells.

Gweep looks in the bowl. "This bad."

Tim looks at the yummy, wobbly, green jelly. <u>"It's really very nice."</u>

Tears form in Gweep's three round eyes. "It's saying no!"

<u>"The slime isn't saying no. It's shaking because it's scared of you."</u>

"Is it scared?" Gweep smiles. "Of me?"

1 because it is wobbly and green, just like slime
2 he smiles because he thinks the jelly is scared of him

Week 10, Day 3
Pg 54

1 Check for correct spelling of each word.
2 a tries **b** spies **c** babies **d** cities **e** carries
3 a ladies **b** babies **c** cries

Week 10, Day 4
Pg 55

1 a carries **b** babies **c** stories **d** parties **e** worries **f** studies
2 Check for correct spelling of each word.
3 a injuries **b** difficulties **c** factories **d** multiplies
4 difficulties, enemies, factories, injuries, libraries, memories, multiplies, properties, qualities, supplies

Week 10, Day 5
Pg 56

1 a rides **b** brushes **c** eats **d** skips **e** bakes

2 a cook **b** buys **c** carry **d** writes **e** dives

3 a play/beat **b** write/draw **c** stop **d** hit **e** eat

Week 11, Day 1
Pg 57

Beds Are Not Trampolines

Tim did a star jump. Then he fell off the bed and landed on his nose. He started to cry.

He cried louder and louder. Mum came running into the room and picked him up.

"Now what have you done?" she asked, looking at his red nose.

"Mandy made me do it," Tim sobbed.

1 b **2** d **3** b **4** d

Week 11, Day 2
Pg 58

Big Trouble

Tim was in big trouble. He had climbed out our bedroom window to fill a water balloon.

As he turned the water on, his balloon flew off. Water sprayed all over the yard. Just then, Mum and Aunt Beth stepped into the garden. Both of them were sprayed with water. Boy, were they angry!

Answers will vary. Suggested answers:

1 surprised

2 Drawing with Tim looking surprised, Mum and Aunt Beth are both angry.

Week 11, Day 3
Pg 59

1 Check for correct spelling of each word.

2 a jewel **b** jump **c** giraffe **d** jug

3 j: jar, jog, jug, joke, jump, jelly, join, June, July, jewel, Japan, adjust, January

g: gem, germ, giant, angel, giraffe, magic, energy

Week 11, Day 4
Pg 60

1 a jump **b** giraffe **c** January **d** jug **e** joke

2 Check for correct spelling of each word.

3 a jacket **b** juice **c** engine **d** jigsaw **e** digit

4 agile, allergy, digit, engine, fragile, jacket, jigsaw, juice, margin, urgent

Week 11, Day 5
Pg 61

1 argue, arrive, mow, hear, imagine

2 go, is, see, try, bites

3 a talks, talk

b live, lives

c runs, run

d drive, drives

e likes, like

Week 12, Day 1
Pg 62

Gee-Gee?

When I picked him up, Greedy Guts chewed on my fingers. Then he gnawed the strap of my watch.

I put him on the floor and he untied my shoelaces. Then he tried to pull my left sock off. He loved me so much, he wanted to eat me. How could I resist him?

"Mum, please," I begged. "He's perfect."

1 c **2** c, d

Week 12, Day 2
Pg 63

Yesterday was Mum's birthday. Aunt Minnie sent Mum a pink, fluffy jacket. Mum hates pink and she hates fluffy.

"I must ring her to say thank you," Mum said. "Aunt Minnie is a dear to remember my birthday, even if she doesn't remember what I like," Mum said.

"Aunt Minnie is family and you can't choose your family. Mmmm ... perhaps I could wash it and say that it shrank."

1 Mum/her birthday

2 a "Aunt Minnie is a dear to remember my birthday, even if she doesn't remember what I like."

b "Perhaps I could wash it and say that it shrank."

Week 12, Day 3
Pg 64

1 Check for correct spelling of each word.

2 el: angel, novel, travel, panel, level, camel, tunnel, kennel, cruel, parcel, towel, label

le: handle, noodle, puddle, title, dimple

al: oval, total, signal

3 a noodle **b** parcel **c** handle **d** kennel

Week 12, Day 4
Pg 65

1 a parcal parcel **b** puddel puddle **c** towl towel **d** dimpl dimple **e** travl travel

2 Check for correct spelling of each word.

3 a buckle **b** shovel **c** cereal **d** people

4 a double **b** hospital **c** turtle

Week 12, Day 5
Pg 66

1 a . **b** ? **c** ? **d** . **e** ? **f** . **g** . **h** ?

2 *Answers will vary. Suggested answer:* Eddie is planting a flower.

3 *Answers will vary. Suggested answer:* I wonder what's inside this box?

Week 13, Day 1
Pg 67

A dog had a fresh, meaty bone, which a butcher had thrown to him. He was heading home with his wonderful bone, as fast as he could go.

1 a **2** b **3** b, d **4** d

Week 13, Day 2
Pg 68

As the dog crossed a bridge over a pond, he looked down and saw himself reflected in the quiet water. The image was like looking in a mirror.

But the dog thought he saw a real dog carrying another bone—a bone much bigger than his! Without thinking, the dog dropped his bone and leapt at the dog in the pond.

1 c

2 quiet, like looking in a mirror

3 d

4 *Answers will vary. Suggested answers:* mirrors, windows, shiny surfaces

5 the same

Week 13, Day 3
Pg 69

1 Check for correct spelling of each word.

2 **a** whorld world **b** whash wash **c** wite white **d** whorm worm **e** wich which

3 Missing letters are underlined
a world **b** witch **c** what **d** wheel/where **e** wipe **f** wall/want **g** wheel/where **h** went/well

Week 13, Day 4
Pg 70

1 **a** whale **b** wheat **c** worm **d** watch

2 Check for correct spelling of each word.

3 **a** whisk **b** wagon **c** wardrobe **d** whistle **e** weather

4 *Answers will vary. Suggested answers*: ward, robe, raw, row, rob, bored, draw, drew

Week 13, Day 5
Pg 71

1 **a** am **b** are **c** was **d** being **e** were
2 **a** is **b** was **c** are **d** am **e** were
3 **a** has **b** have **c** had

Week 14, Day 1
Pg 72

Berries to Jam

Berries can be eaten fresh. They can also be cooked with sugar to make jam.

1. Berries grow on small bushes or plants in fields and greenhouses.
2. Some farmers use machines to harvest the ripe berries. Others are picked by hand.
3. The berries are washed, trimmed and cut up or mashed. Then, the berries are cooked with sugar until the mixture is thick.
4. Next, the hot jam is poured into jars and sealed to keep it fresh.

1 They are grown on small bushes or plants.

2 They are cooked with sugar until the mixture is thick.

3 into jars

4 the numbers next to each step

Week 14, Day 2
Pg 73

1 Then/Next/After this, Finally

2 *Suggested answer:* cows in shed, milking the cows, milk tanker, boiling the milk, milk in bottles, shop or supermarket

Week 14, Day 3
Pg 74

1 Check for correct spelling of each word.

2 **a** door **b** poor **c** after **d** even **e** hold

3 **a** sugar **b** hour **c** half **d** child

Week 14, Day 4
Pg 75

1 after, again, bath, child, climb, door, even, father, grass, great, half, hold, hour, past, poor, pretty, prove, sugar, sure, who

2 Check for correct spelling of each word.

3 **a** stek steak **b** butiful beautiful **c** wole whole **d** everibody everybody **e** cloes clothes

4 *Answers will vary. Read through sentence together.*

Week 14, Day 5
Pg 76

1 present tense: push, sail, fill, play
past tense: walked, stopped, blamed, picked

2 **a** fix, fixed
b enter, entered
c finish, finished
d visit, visited
e watch, watched

3 **a** Yesterday I locked the door to the garage.
b Last night I washed the dishes after dinner.

Week 15, Day 1
Pg 77

1 ✔ c, d, f ✘ a, b, e

2 pens and hammers

3 hammers and pens

4 a calculator

5 blenders and calculators

Week 15, Day 2
Pg 78

1970s

Many new tools and gadgets became popular in the 1970s.

Prior to the 1970s, most schools used books, blackboards and paper as educational tools.

By the 1970s, many schools had film projectors, record players and tape recorders to help children learn.

By the late 1970s, people began to buy personal computers for their homes.

1

School Tool	Used before 1970	Used in the 1970s	Used today
Books	✔	✔	✔
Blackboards	✔	✔	✘
Paper and pencils	✔	✔	✔
Film projectors	✘	✔	✘
Record players	✘	✔	✘
Tape recorders	✘	✔	✘

2 books, blackboards, paper and pencils

3 books, paper and pencils

Week 15, Day 3
Pg 79

1 Check for correct spelling of each word.

2 **a** olive, olives **b** leaf, leaves **c** hive, hives **d** scarf, scarves

3 **a** gloves **b** giraffes **c** shelves

Week 15, Day 4
Pg 80

1 just add s: puffs, safes, reefs, cliffs, waves, stoves, sleeves, hives, olives, gloves, cafes, giraffes
change f to ves: lives, wives, elves, leaves, wolves, loaves, scarves, shelves

2 Check for correct spelling of each word.

3 **a** knives **b** calves **c** grooves **d** halves

4 *Answers will vary. Read through sentence together.*

Week 15, Day 5
Pg 81

1 **a** is **b** am **c** has **d** are **e** have

2 **a** scooting
b singing

3 **a** have, has
b is, are
c was, were

Week 16, Day 1
Pg 82

Transport

Vehicles, such as cars, buses, trains, planes and boats, transport us from one place to another.

Some people use transport to make short, daily trips to work or school. Others use it for longer journeys, such as a holiday or business trip overseas.

Public transport is designed for moving large groups of people. Buses, trains, trams, ferries and planes are types of public transport. Private transport includes cars, motorcycles and bicycles.

1	Purpose	Examples
Private transport	moving small numbers of people	cars, motorcycles and bicycles
Public transport	moving large groups of people	buses, trains, trams, ferries and planes

2 takes people from place to place

Week 16, Day 2
Pg 83

Cars

In the early 1900s, people began to buy their own cars. In 1908, Henry Ford began making cars on an assembly line. His factory made cars at a much faster rate. These mass-produced cars were cheaper to buy.

In the 1950s, many more people owned cars. More cars meant more roads. With more cars on the road, people started to think about car safety. The first seat belts strapped across the driver's lap.

1

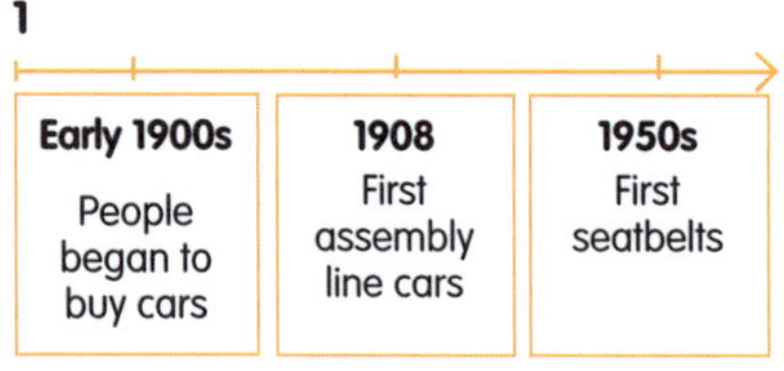

2 a **3** c

Week 16, Day 3
Pg 84

1 Check for correct spelling of each word.

2 a soup **b** fruit **c** shoe **d** suit

3 a ruby **b** shoe **c** fruit **d** prune **e** blue

Week 16, Day 4
Pg 85

1 Missing letters are underlined
a screw **b** clue **c** grew
d crew **e** blue/blew **f** flew
g chew **h** threw **i** soup

2 Check for correct spelling of each word.

3 a could **b** canoe **c** gruesome **d** through

4 a bruise **b** cashew **c** could **d** should

Week 16, Day 5
Pg 86

1 a up the tree/to the treehouse.
b by bus.
c at seven o'clock.

2 a will **b** is **c** am **d** going **e** to

3 a Tomorrow I will/am going to buy a new model plane.
b Next week I will/am going to visit my cousins in Queensland.

Week 17, Day 1
Pg 87

Dear Mum,

Today we got up really early and went to the zoo. It was huge! The giraffes had lots of room and the lions hid in the bushes. Dad pretended to be a mountain goat. We bought ice creams after lunch. Boo-boo had chocolate and I had vanilla. Dad carried us when we got really tired. See you tomorrow!

Love, T

xx

1 *Answers will vary. Check responses.*

2 *Answers will vary. Check responses.*

Week 17, Day 2
Pg 88

Dear Anna and Janek,

We arrived in Paris yesterday afternoon. Last night we went up to the top of the Eiffel Tower. The city was all lit up and so pretty. Today we went to three art galleries, so I have sore feet! What have you been doing?

Love, Vicky and Sean

1 a card you write about your holiday

2 to tell their friends and family about their holidays

3 where they are, what they've seen, how they feel

4 *Answers will vary. Check postcard has a greeting, details of a holiday and a sign-off.*

Week 17, Day 3
Pg 89

1 Check for correct spelling of each word.

2 ful: awful, helpful, spoonful, plateful, handful, thankful, forgetful, powerful, cheerful, joyful, playful, mouthful, graceful, grateful, spiteful, truthful
less: useless, careless, restless, harmless

Week 17, Day 4
Pg 90

1 a spoonfull spoonful
b platefull plateful
c careles careless
d truthfull truthful

2 Check for correct spelling of each word.

3 a plentiful **b** colourless **c** wonderful **d** disgraceful

4 *Answers will vary. Read through sentence together.*

Week 17, Day 5
Pg 91

1 a fought **b** shining **c** divided
d yawned **e** ate **f** wrote
g held

2 a bravely **b** brightly **c** equally
d sleepily **e** greedily **f** neatly
g tightly

3 *Answers will vary. Possible answers include:*
a politely **b** correctly **c** loudly
d quickly

Week 18, Day 1
Pg 92

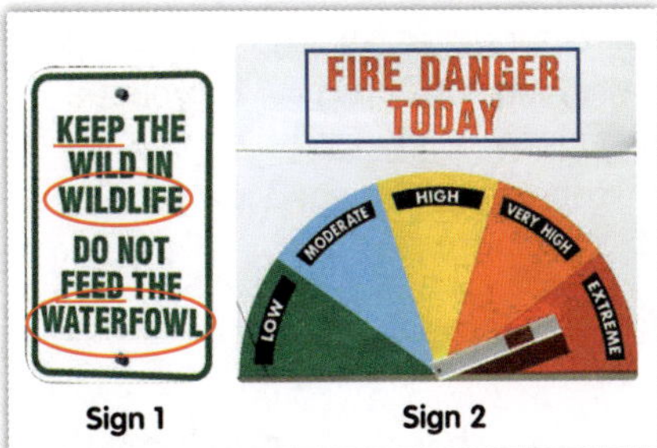

1 a live in the wild
b live in the water some of the time
2 a extreme **b** severe **c** low

Week 18, Day 2
Pg 93

1 easy to break
2 Handle with care and the pictures
3 the contents can be broken, handle with care
4 *Answers will vary. Suggested answers:* glass, crystal, porcelain
5 *Answers will vary. Suggested answer:* on a package of crystal glasses

Week 18, Day 3
Pg 94

1 Check for correct spelling of each word.
2 a gnome **b** knife **c** knot **d** write
3 a write **b** kneel **c** gnash

Week 18, Day 4
Pg 95

1 a knock **b** knelt **c** knot **d** wrist
2 Check for correct spelling of each word.
3 a knuckle **b** wriggle **c** knight **d** wreckage **e** knead
4 *Answers will vary. Read through story together.*

Week 18, Day 5
Pg 96

1 a . **b** ! **c** ! **d** . **e** . **f** !/.
2 a How brilliant was that!
b How exciting is this!
3 a What a cute puppy that is!
b What an exciting ride that was!

REVIEW 2
Spelling
Pg 97

1 Missing letters are underlined
a tow<u>el</u> **b** ov<u>al</u> **c** pudd<u>le</u>
2 c
3 Missing letters are underlined
a <u>k</u>nob **b** <u>w</u>rist **c** <u>wh</u>ale **d** <u>g</u>nash
4 a
5 a parties **b** rubies **c** scarves **d** cafes

Grammar
Pg 98–99

1 a run **b** catch
2 a <u>cook</u> cooked **b** <u>wash</u> washed
3 a ? **b** .
4 a is **b** am **c** have
5 a am **b** are
6 a ~~were~~ was **b** ~~are~~ is
7 will **b** am
8 a early
b quickly
c smoothly
9 a ! **b** .

Comprehension
100–101

1 b **2** c **3** a **4** c **5** b **6** d
7 c **8** a **9** d **10** b

Week 19, Day 1
Pg 102

Imagine This, Imagine That

"It's easy. One person starts imagining something that doesn't exist, say a flying car and the next person has to add to it," said Luke.
"So you could imagine a flying car shaped like a fish," said Aunt Stella.
Sophie understood. "And the flying car shaped like a fish could spray fireworks from its wheels."

1 a
2 b
3 d

Week 19, Day 2
Pg 103

Art Eyes

"Look out for colours, patterns, shapes, textures and shadows that catch your attention. Draw them in your journal and collect as much treasure as you can!" Aunt Stella cried.
Sophie liked the shapes and colours of the shells. She collected lots of shells of all shapes, sizes, colours and patterns.
Sophie also rubbed some rock textures into her journal and drew a rough sketch of the beach. But her most precious find was a piece of blue, weathered glass.

1 shells
2 a sketch of the beach
3 precious
4 *Answers will vary. Suggested answer:* One day I found a beautiful peacock's feather. I took it home and put it in a jar. It's the most precious thing I have.

Week 19, Day 3
Pg 104

1 Check for correct spelling of each word.
2 est: finest, loudest, neatest, newest, coldest, thickest, fullest, smallest, clearest
er: paler, duller, nicer, fewer, later, cuter, whiter, fresher, prouder, steeper, sharper
3 a <u>smalest</u> smallest **b** <u>coouter</u> cuter
c <u>steper</u> steeper

Week 19, Day 4
Pg 105

1 a sharper **b** nicer **c** paler
d fresher **e** neatest
2 Check for correct spelling of each word.
3 a younger **b** brightest **c** straighter
d fiercer **e** higher
4 *Answers will vary. Read through sentences together.*

Week 19, Day 5
Pg 106

1 a cat **b** bird **c** Ruby **d** Liam
e baby **f** book **g** Sam **h** frog
i Mandy **j** monkey
2 Tick: a, d, e
3 a Alex is wearing Jose's goggles.
b Dad's car is in the garage.
c My grandpa's glasses are on the table.
d The boy's lunch is in his bag.
e The child's T-shirt is covered in mud.
f Ben's kitten is very playful.

Week 20, Day 1
Pg 107

Smelly and Stuck

Jake's toenail went PING! Jake spun around like a corkscrew. And there he stuck.

Everybody pushed and shoved. People with cameras took photos. People with notebooks asked questions.

"What does it feel like to be trapped by your toenail, Jake? they asked.

The sacks were full of fertiliser. The longest toenail in the world was no fun anymore.

1 b 2 c 3 a 4 b

Week 20, Day 2
Pg 108

Sam's Cool Idea

The longest toenail in the world was growing.

Longer and wider and taller! And it was growing FAST!

It curled three times round his body. It shot past his ears. It twisted over his head. It snaked up past the diving board.

Jake gasped as his toenail snaked and grew. As big as himself ... as tall as a tree ... as big as a house ... as tall as a crane.

1 *Answers will vary. Suggested answer:* a drawing of a boy with a very long toenail.

2 *Answers will vary. Suggested answer:* I would feel excited to be different to everyone else.

3 Jake gasped

Week 20, Day 3
Pg 109

1 Check for correct spelling of each word.

2 **a** flea **b** hole **c** toe **d** plane **e** sail **f** rain **g** meat **h** steal

3 **a** plane **b** hole **c** sail **d** sale **e** steal

Week 20, Day 4
Pg 110

1 **a** flea **b** whole **c** steel **d** flee **e** prey

2 Check for correct spelling of each word.

3 **a** morning **b** rays **c** higher **d** hall **e** where

4 *Answers will vary. Read through sentences together.*

Week 20, Day 5
Pg 111

1 **a** mine **b** our **c** her **d** your **e** my **f** their

2 **a** his **b** your **c** mine **d** ours **e** their

3 **a** my **b** its **c** theirs **d** mine

Week 21, Day 1
Pg 112

The Home Haircut

"Easy," said Jan as she cut. "Piece of cake!"

I remember when Jan said cooking was easy. We spent an afternoon scraping burnt food off the stove.

Jan also told me that camping was easy. The tent fell on top of us during the night.

By three o'clock on Saturday afternoon there was more hair on the bathroom floor than on my head.

1 c

2 c

3 a

Week 21, Day 2
Pg 113

The Home Haircut

"Look in the mirror, Freya," said Jan.

I did. There was a lot of face and not much hair.

"Is it all right?" Jan said, looking worried.

"One side is longer than the other," I said softly.

Jan cut some more. Snip. Snip. Snip.

In the mirror, I looked strange. My hair was gone. Bits stuck out all over the place.

Jan's face was white.

1 she doesn't like it

2 she says, "I looked strange."

3 *Answers will vary. Suggested answer:* Drawing of Freya with short, uneven hair and Jan looking very nervous.

Week 21, Day 3
Pg 114

1 Check for correct spelling of each word.

2 ing: jogging, wagging, stopping, bobbing, gripping, trapping

ed: rubbed, jogged, sagged, sipped, rammed, tipped, thinned, planned, stabbed, grabbed, stopped, blotted, skinned, flopped

3 **a** jogging **b** jogged **c** grabbed **d** bobbing

Week 21, Day 4
Pg 115

1 Check for correct spelling of each word.

2 **a** shipped **b** knitting **c** throbbed **d** stunned **e** squatted

3 **a** scanning **b** shrugged **c** scrubbing **d** strapping **e** prodding

Week 21, Day 5
Pg 116

1 **a** asked **b** replied **c** exclaimed **d** shrieked **e** sobbed **f** grumbled **g** yelled

2 **a** gasped **b** cheered **c** greeted **d** begged **e** warned **f** complained **g** whispered

Week 22, Day 1
Pg 117

Ringmaster Roy: Chuckles, perhaps you could teach Snoz about being a clown.

Narrator: Chuckles had a great time dressing Snoz and painting him with make-up. But when Snoz saw himself in the mirror, he hid under the table.

Snoz: Not funny! Too scary! Snoz is scared!

Narrator: Snoz began to cry. Seeing a Snozalot cry made Chuckles cry too.

Chuckles: (sobbing) That is the saddest thing I have ever seen. A sobbing Snozalot!

1 a

2 b, c

Week 22, Day 2
Pg 118

Ringmaster Roy: Tell me troupe, what can Snoz the Snozalot Monster do?

Chuckles: I will tell you what he cannot do. He cannot make you laugh.

Bendy Betty: He cannot bend.

Max Manyhands: He cannot juggle.

Ringmaster Roy: I see, I see. I see. And I know he can't fly through the air.

Chuckles: He's a nice monster.

Bendy Betty: A lovely monster, really.

Max Manyhands: But Snoz has no place in Circus Bizurkus.

1 Snoz the Snozalot Monster/Circus Bizurkus

2 **a** do circus acts.

b no place in Circus Bizurkus.

Week 22, Day 3
Pg 119

1 Check for correct spelling of each word.
2 a beak **b** rock **c** mask **d** trunk
3 ck words: lock, rock, tick, luck, peck, track, pluck, check, stick, shack, stock
k words: beak, bank, tank, pink, dusk, cheek, mask, speak, trunk

Week 22, Day 4
Pg 120

1 a bank **b** pink **c** dusk
2 Check for correct spelling of each word.
3 a cloak **b** stork **c** chipmunk **d** crook
4 a soak **b** thank **c** cloak **d** chipmunk

Week 22, Day 5
Pg 121

1 a "How many pets have you got?"
b "I'll wait for you outside."
c "How good was that!"
d "Come here at once!"
e "I wish I had a pet guinea pig."
f "Now, what have I done with my purse?"
2 a "How are you feeling today?" asked the doctor.
b "I would like porridge for breakfast," said the child.
c "What a large bear!" gasped Victoria.
d "Don't go too near the edge," warned the ranger.
e "I will never do that again," promised Ethan.
3 *Answers will vary. Suggested answer:* "I am 7 years old," said Adam.

Week 23, Day 1
Pg 122

The gnat dived at the lion and stung him on the nose. The lion was furious. He swiped at the gnat, but only ended up scratching himself with his sharp claws. The gnat attacked the lion again and again and the lion raged.

1 d
2 a, e
3 d

Week 23, Day 2
Pg 123

Finally, the lion was worn out. He was dripping with blood from his own scratches and he lay down, defeated by the gnat. The gnat buzzed away to tell the whole Animal Kingdom about his victory over the lion, but instead he flew straight into a spider's web.

1 b
2 a defeated by the gnat
b worn out the lion
3 Don't be too quick to claim victory.

Week 23, Day 3
Pg 124

1 Check for correct spelling of each word.

2

quick	quickly
strong	strongly
most	mostly
nice	nicely

3 a easly easily
b quikly quickly
c softy softly
d sudenly suddenly
e slowlee slowly

Week 23, Day 4
Pg 125

1 badly, calmly, clearly, easily, fairly, firmly, gently, happily, largely, mainly, mostly, nicely, quickly, quietly, shyly, slowly, softly, strongly, suddenly, swiftly
2 Check for correct spelling of each word.
3 a equally
b finally
c completely
d slightly
4 *Answers will vary. Read through sentence together.*

Week 23, Day 5
Pg 126

1 *Answers will vary. Ask for an explanation.*
2 a ! **b** ? **c** ?
d ! **e** ?
3 *Answers will vary. Suggested answers:*
What stung my face?
I live in a house.

Week 24, Day 1
Pg 127

Finding Fossils

Places where rocks are eroding might have fossils. Creek banks, dry riverbeds and cliff faces are all good places to look. Most fossils are covered by a thick layer of rock. At some sites, explosives blow up the rock and bulldozers cart it away. Often the whole block of rock, with its bones, is cut out. This is taken back to the lab where the bones are carefully removed.

1 5, 3, 2, 4, 6, 1
2 museum

Week 24, Day 2
Pg 128

Giant Jigsaw Puzzles

Putting a dinosaur back together takes skill, patience and a lot of time.

Using photos and drawings, the skeleton is laid out on the floor and then put back together from the ground up.

Most bones are too fragile to become a skeleton in a museum. A plaster or plastic cast is made. It is rare to find a complete skeleton—most museums' dinosaurs are put together with extra parts.

1 *Answers will vary. Suggested answer:* Drawings of the bones. Skeleton on the floor. Making a cast. Skeleton put together.

Week 24, Day 3
Pg 129

1 Check for correct spelling of each word.
2 a badge **b** orange **c** bridge
d hedge **e** judge
3 a smudge **b** strange **c** image
d orange **e** hedge

Week 24, Day 4
Pg 130

1 a plunge **b** change **c** fringe
d village **e** charge **f** garage
2 Check for correct spelling of each word.
3 a cottage **b** package **c** courage
d partridge **e** sausage
4 a damage **b** passage **c** package

Week 24, Day 5
Pg 131

1 a always **b** already **c** tomorrow **d** later/tomorrow **e** weekly/tomorrow

2 a hourly **b** regularly **c** never **d** earlier **e** now **f** sometimes **g** tonight

3 *Answers will vary. Suggested answer:* Yesterday I went to the beach.

Week 25, Day 1
Pg 132

A World-changing Gizmo

It all began in 1947. That's when three scientists invented the transistor. The three scientists were from the Bell Laboratories. Their names were John Bardeen, Walter Brattain and William Shockley.

The first transistor was about the size of your thumb. It was made from a paperclip, gold foil, wire and a bit of plastic. Transistors were first used in telephones.

Transistors are in computers, the Internet, mobile phones, TVs, video cameras, calculators, hand-held games, radar, satellites and night vision technology.

1 c
2 b
3 b

Week 25, Day 2
Pg 133

Why Didn't I Think of That?

Dr Nakamatsu is a modern inventor. He holds the world record for the most patents and inventions. Dr Nakamatsu has over 3200 inventions.

Dr Nakamatsu often came up with ideas underwater. He invented a notepad that he could use underwater to write down his ideas.

Dr Nakamatsu only sleeps four hours a night. He says the best time for new ideas is between midnight and 4 am. He has two special rooms that help him think.

1 He had ideas underwater but couldn't write them down.

2 He invented a notepad that he could use underwater.

3 *Answers will vary. Read through answers together.*

Week 25, Day 3
Pg 134

1 Check for correct spelling of each word.

2 a starfish **b** hairbrush **c** raincoat **d** pancake

Week 25, Day 4
Pg 135

1 a Strawbery Strawberry
b snoman snowman
c raincote raincoat
d bakpack backpack
e harebrush hairbrush

2 Check for correct spelling of each word.

3 a watermelon **b** outside **c** marketplace **d** doughnut

4 a watermelon **b** clockwork

Week 25, Day 5
Pg 136

1 a barbecue **b** umbrella **c** lolly **d** man **e** truck **f** mice **g** day **h** bat **i** shape

2 a fluffy **b** juicy **c** electric **d** tiny **e** new **f** dirty

Week 26, Day 1
Pg 137

1

	Travels on and between					Travel for			Time ...		On board		
	rivers	harbours	lakes	cities	countries	work	holiday	school	minutes or hours	days or weeks	shops	movie theaters	bathrooms
ferry	✔	✔	✔	✔	✔	✔		✔	✔				✔
cruise ship				✔	✔		✔			✔	✔	✔	✔

2 bathrooms

3 cities and countries

Week 26, Day 2
Pg 138

1

Boat	What does it do?	How many people	Interesting fact
destroyer	protects bigger, slower ships	300	moves fast
submarine	travels underwater	150	moves fast
aircraft carrier	carries planes	5000	biggest ship in the Navy

2 They are all navy vessels.

Week 26, Day 3
Pg 139

1 Check for correct spelling of each word.

2 a h'es he's **b** cant' can't **c** she'l she'll **d** Im I'm **e** I'ts It's

3 a where's **b** didn't **c** I've **d** how's

Week 26, Day 4
Pg 140

1 a it'll **b** we'll **c** won't **d** you'd

2 Check for correct spelling of each word.

3 a weren't **b** would've **c** doesn't **d** wasn't **e** couldn't **f** you're

4 a wasn't **b** mustn't **c** couldn't **d** o'clock

Week 26, Day 5
Pg 141

1 a or **b** and **c** so **d** nor **e** but

2 a and **b** nor **c** so **d** so **e** or, but

3 *Answers will vary. Suggested answers:*
a I like apples and bananas.
b I looked under my bed but my socks were not under there.
c We can go to the park, or to the beach.

Week 27, Day 1
Pg 142

Hoofed Mammals

Hoofed mammals eat plants. They are herbivores. Zebras, giraffes and elephants are all hoofed mammals.

Many hoofed mammals live in groups called herds. They often live on open plains or grasslands. The herd moves from place to place in search of food. Zebras and wildebeests live in large herds.

Elephants are the largest land animals. They live in family groups called herds. Baby elephants feed on mother's milk for two years while they grow.

1 d **2** c

Week 27, Day 2
Pg 143

Monkeys and Apes

Monkeys and apes are mammals called primates. They are warm-blooded, furry animals that suckle their young.

Baboons, mandrills and howlers are all monkeys. Monkeys are very good climbers. They use their hands, feet and tails to help them climb.

Apes are larger than monkeys. Chimpanzees, gibbons, orangutans and gorillas are all apes. Apes do not have tails.

Gorillas are the largest of all the apes and are tailless. They live in family groups.

1

small	larger	largest
Monkeys (baboons, mandrills and howlers)	Apes (chimpanzees, gibbons and orangutans)	Gorillas

2 Monkeys have tails but apes don't.

3 "Apes do not have tails."

Week 27, Day 3
Pg 144

1 Check for correct spelling of each word.
2 a spider, spiders b bee, bees
c dish, dishes d book, books
e lion, lions f eye, eyes
g shark, sharks h lamb, lambs

Week 27, Day 4
Pg 145

1 a pigs b lions c bees d coats
e books f bunches
2 Check for correct spelling of each word.
3 a giraffes b flowers c fingers
d oranges
4 a monkeys b fingers

Week 27, Day 5
Pg 146

1 a hasn't b can't c I've d isn't
e aren't
2 a i b a c o d ha
3 a they'll b didn't c that's d haven't
e doesn't

REVIEW 3
Spelling
Pg 147

1 a spiders b branches
2 c 3 a k b dge
4 a who's b would've
5 a 6 pancake
7 b 8 kniting knitting

Grammar
Pg 148–149

1 a Dan's b baby's
2 a hers yours b Their mine
3 a yelled b whispered
4 a "How many lollies have you had?" asked Joey.
b "Not half as many as you," replied Ella.
5 a nor b but
c so d or
6 a later b immediately
7 a squirrels b table
8 a . b ?
9 a We'll b It's

Comprehension
Pg 150–151

1 d 2 b 3 b 4 b 5 c 6 c
7 a 8 b 9 c 10 b

Week 28, Day 1
Pg 152

The Sniffles

Vinnie raced in the front door. His bag skidded across the living room floor.

"What's going on in here?" Vinnie's mum stood in the doorway, hands on her hips.

Vinnie walked over and picked up his bag.

"Sorry, Mum. I'm in a bit of a hurry."

"What about a snack?"

"I'm not hungry."

Mary stood in shock as she watched him run up the stairs.

1 a 2 b, c 3 c

Week 28, Day 2
Pg 153

Dr Hacker

Vinnie pulled the ad from his pocket and dialled the number.

"Hello," said the voice on the other end of the line.

"Are you Dr Hacker?" asked Vinnie.

"That's right."

Vinnie explained his problem.

"Never fear, young Vinnie. I'll be there in a flash," said Dr Hacker.

Vinnie hung up. Smoke filled the hall and a flash of light blinded him.

Dr Hacker waved away the smoke.

"Show me your sick computer."

1 It's a computer problem.
2 He is magical.
3 The text says, "Smoke filled the hall and a flash of light blinded him."

Week 28, Day 3
Pg 154

1 Check for correct spelling of each word.
2 a became b bound c sprang
d fought e swung f awoke
3 Missing letters are underlined
a did b clung c chose d froze
e stole
4 a awake awoke b shake shook
c eat ate d give gave e forget forgot

Week 28, Day 4
Pg 155

1 Check for correct spelling of each word.
2 a brought b taught c struck
d understood e caught
3 a caught b shrank c brought
d struck e taught f built

Week 28, Day 5
Pg 156

1 a thought b bought c fell
d brought e went f felt
2 a gave b ate c was
d won e stole f began
g had
3 a knew b told c sat
d wrote e flew f saw
g made h taught

Week 29, Day 1
Pg 157

1 b, d
2 c

Week 29, Day 2
Pg 158

1 *Answers will vary. Read answers together.*
2 *Answers will vary. Read answers together.*
3 *Answers will vary. Discuss pictures together.*

Week 29, Day 3
Pg 159

1 Check for correct spelling of each word.
2 a smile b plate c bone d nine
3 a bone b smile c plate d stone
e blade f nine
4

a–e	e–e	i–e	o–e	u–e
face	these	nine	bone	June
safe		smile	close	rule
plate		glide	stone	prune
skate		slide	alone	
blade			stole	
shade			whole	

Week 29, Day 4
Pg 160

1 Check for correct spelling of each word.
2 a crocodile b lemonade c tadpole
d whale e microwave
3 a scrape b shave c tadpole
d gnome

Week 29, Day 5
Pg 161

1 a to **b** out **c** past **d** beside
e with **f** of **g** in
2 a at **b** past **c** above **d** on
e under **f** for **g** in
3 on, in, on

Week 30, Day 1
Pg 162

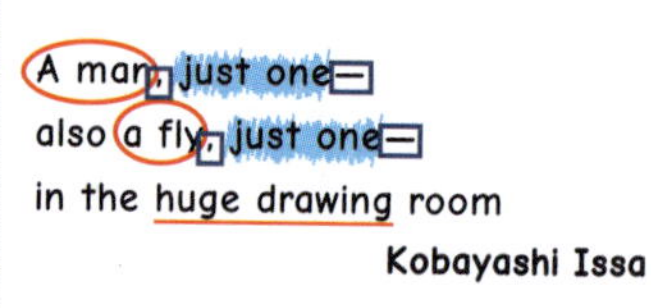
A man, just one—
also a fly, just one—
in the huge drawing room
Kobayashi Issa

1 a, d **2** b, d **3** b **4** b

Week 30, Day 2
Pg 163

Warm snug speckled egg
Dappled light fading quickly
Soft crack of split shell
Alysha Hodge

1 d **2** d **3** c **4** d

Week 30, Day 3
Pg 164

1 Check for correct spelling of each word.
2 ee words: meet, feet, greet, fleet, sheet, sweet, tweet, street
ea words: meat, heat, seat, beat, neat, treat, cheat, pleat, wheat, bleat, upbeat, repeat
3 a greet **b** sheet **c** feet **d** street

Week 30, Day 4
Pg 165

1 a fleet **b** bleat **c** beat **d** tweet
e wheat
2 Check for correct spelling of each word.
3 a overeat **b** retreat **c** athlete
d parakeet
4 a compete **b** complete **c** heartbeat

Week 30, Day 5
Pg 166

1 a against **b** in **c** since **d** with
2 a when **b** where **c** how **d** when
e how
3 a at **b** by **c** to **d** in

Week 31, Day 1
Pg 167

A hungry fox was looking for food. She saw bunches of juicy, plump grapes growing high up on a farmer's fence.
"I will have those grapes. I'm starving!" she said.

1 d **2** b, d **3** b

Week 31, Day 2
Pg 168

The fox ran at the fence and leapt as high as she could. It was a great leap—but it wasn't high enough. She hadn't even reached the lowest bunch of grapes.
The fox tried again. She ran and leapt and it was another wonderful leap. But once again, she did not jump high enough to reach the fruit. She didn't give up though.

1 b
2 a but it wasn't high enough
b again but it wasn't high enough

Week 31, Day 3
Pg 169

1 Check for correct spelling of each word.
a tractor **b** saucer **c** doctor **d** spider
3 a dinner **b** cracker **c** brother **d** saucer
e finger **f** tractor
4 a enter **b** together **c** mirror
d another **e** wander **f** pepper

Week 31, Day 4
Pg 170

1 a docter doctor **b** peppor pepper
c doller dollar **d** mirrar mirror
e wandor wander
2 Check for correct spelling of each word.
3 a alligator **b** September **c** November
d feather
4 *Answers will vary. Read through story together.*

Week 31, Day 5
Pg 171

1 Tick: a, d, e
2 *Answers will vary. Read through sentences.*
3 a Are they having lunch?
b Is the monkey swinging in the tree?

Week 32, Day 1
Pg 172

Bengal Tigers
Some Bengal tigers live in the mangrove forests of India and Bangladesh.
Tigers hunt mammals, such as wild boars. Bengal tigers also eat saltwater crabs and fish.
Tigers are quick and powerful hunters. They have soft foot pads that help them quietly stalk prey. Their striped coats help tigers hide in the forest. Every tiger has a different pattern of stripes.

1 d
2 a, b, d
3 Drawing of a wild boar, crab and fish.

Week 32, Day 2
Pg 173

Hippopotamuses
Hippos live in swampy lakes and rivers in Africa.
Hippos spend the day in the water. A hippo's eyes, ears and nostrils are on the top of its head. It can watch for danger while the rest of its body is underwater.
Hippos nurse their young and even sleep underwater. Hippos do not truly swim. They run or walk along the river bed.
Hippos are often aggressive. They open their mouths to warn off intruders.

1 Drawing of a labelled hippopotamus

Week 32, Day 3
Pg 174

1 Check for correct spelling of each word.
2 a maid **b** decade **c** spade **d** aid
e raid
3 Missing letters are underlined
a invade **b** blade **c** wade
d sunshade **e** trade **f** arcade
4 afraid, aid, arcade, blade, decade, fade, grade, invade, laid, made, maid, paid, parade, raid, shade, spade, sunshade, trade, upgrade, wade

Week 32, Day 4
Pg 175

1 Check for correct spelling of each word.
2 a braid **b** marmalade
c bridesmaid **d** lemonade **e** persuade
3 a cascade **b** grenade **c** persuade

Week 32, Day 5
Pg 176

1 a . **b** ? **c** ! **d** . **e** ?
2 Tick: a, c, e
3 a I have a dog and a cat.
b How old are you today?

Week 33, Day 1
Pg 177

1

Vegetable	Cooler weather	Warmer weather	Quick to grow	Longer to grow
carrot	✔			✔
corn		✔		✔
capsicum		✔	✔	
onion	✔			✔
winter lettuce	✔		✔	
tomato		✔		✔

2 c, d, e

Week 33, Day 2
Pg 178

Cows and Sheep

Some farmers raise large herds of cattle. Others raise large flocks of sheep.

Farmers raise herds of cows, called cattle, for their meat and hides. Leather is made into shoes, clothes and furniture. Cattle eat grass in fields or are fed hay and grain.

Dairy cows make milk. Milk can be made into cheese, yogurt and ice cream.

Farmers raise sheep for their wool, meat and milk. Farmers shear sheep once a year. The wool can be made into sweaters, blankets and carpets.

1

Week 33, Day 3
Pg 179

1 Check for correct spelling of each word.

2

happy	watch	begin
happiness	watching	beginning
happily	watched	beginner
happiest	watchful	began

3 a law **b** unlawful **c** fright **d** frightened
e watching

Week 33, Day 4
Pg 180

1 a watched **b** watchful **c** happiness
d beginning **e** beginner **f** fright
2 Check for correct spelling of each word.
3 a garden **b** deciding **c** gardener
d friendly **e** decide
4 *Answers will vary. Read through story together.*

Week 33, Day 5
Pg 181

1 a and **b** so **c** and **d** or **e** but
2 a fed, and, bathed **b** packed, but, left
c was, so, stayed **d** Drink, or, put
3 a Max plays basketball and Abby plays baseball.
b Jackson is tall but Joshua is taller.

Week 34, Day 1
Pg 182

How a jet engine works

Jet engines burn a mixture of fuel and air. This makes hot gases, which give thrust. Thrust gets a plane off the ground and keeps it moving.

1 b **2** 3, 4, 1, 5, 2

Week 34, Day 2
Pg 183

Swing Wings

Wide wings help get a plane off the ground. They also slow it down in the sky. Swing wings solve this problem. On fighters like the F-14 Tomcat, the wings sweep back once the jet is in the air.

1 the wide wings
2 out to the sides
3 after take-off
4 they swing out to the sides again

Week 34, Day 3
Pg 184

1 Check for correct spelling of each word.
2 er: bigger, tinier, easier, heavier, happier, healthier, angrier, flatter, funnier
est: biggest, fattest, tiniest, easiest, saddest, heaviest, happiest, healthiest, angriest, busiest, funniest

Week 34, Day 4
Pg 185

1 a bigger **b** funniest **c** biggest
d easiest **e** happiest
2 Check for correct spelling of each word.
3 a fluffier/dirtier **b** dimmer
c curliest/dirtiest **d** tidier/dirtier
4 a smelliest **b** scariest **c** thinnest

Week 34, Day 5
Pg 186

1 a murray **b** everest **c** christmas
d apple **e** melbourne **f** australia
2 a uluru, northern, territory
b ford, toyota
c ravenscliff, public, school
d saint, patrick's, day
e europe, africa, south, america
3 a Max plays basketball and Abby plays baseball.
b Jackson is tall but Joshua is taller.
4 My best friend lives on Simpson Street.

Week 35, Day 1
Pg 187

Healthy Foods

Your body needs a variety of good foods to grow and stay healthy.

The food we eat is called our diet. A balanced diet contains a wide variety of foods.

Carbohydrates in foods such as bread and rice give us energy. Other foods, like fruits and vegetables, are full of vitamins and minerals.

We need protein to make muscles, skin and hair. Meat and eggs are high-protein foods. We need calcium for our teeth and bones. Dairy foods, like cheese and milk, are high in calcium.

1

	Why we need them	Examples
Carbohydrates	give us energy	bread, rice
Fruit and vegetables	full of vitamins and minerals	*Answers will vary.*
Protein	makes muscles, skin and hair	eggs, meat
Dairy	good for teeth and bones	milk, cheese

Week 35, Day 2

Pg 188

Grains

A healthy diet should include grains, such as wheat, rice and corn.

Some grain is cooked and eaten whole. These are wholegrain foods. Other grain is ground into flour to make bread, pasta and cereals. All grains have carbohydrates, which give the body energy.

Some wholegrain foods are corn on the cob, rice and wholegrain bread. They are high in fibre. Wholegrains contain magnesium, a mineral that helps build strong bones and teeth.

1 carbohydrates which the body can use for energy

2 fibre and magnesium

3 building strong bones and teeth

Week 35, Day 3

Pg 189

1 Check for correct spelling of each word.

2 a school b outside c mother d father

3 a off b wanted c pretty d with e outside f always

4 a have b off c around d next

Week 35, Day 4

Pg 190

1 a le I b outsde outside c wantid wanted d weth with e agein again

2 Check for correct spelling of each word.

3 a children b swimming c February d favourite e scared

4 *Answers will vary. Read through sentence together.*

Week 35, Day 5

Pg 191

1 *Answers will vary. Suggested answers:*

a I liked the film because it starred my favourite actor.

b I'm going to the beach because it is hot.

c We're running for the ferry because we are late.

2 a while b because c if d while e because f while g while

Week 36, Day 1

Pg 192

1800s

During the 1800s, machinery for making clothes was invented. More factories were built. Textiles became mass-produced.

Before machinery, weavers and tailors made clothes by hand.

Sewing machines were invented and then mass-produced during the 1800s. This allowed women at home to make clothing quickly and easily. Clothes of the 1800s were often uncomfortable to wear. Women wore bone corsets that laced up tightly.

1 a 2 b, e

Week 36, Day 2

Pg 193

1990s

During the 1990s, people wore shirts, hats and sunglasses to protect against skin cancer.

Hats were not popular in the 1970s and 1980s. In the 1990s, people became more aware of skin cancer. Hats became common again.

Many swimming costumes, especially for young children, once again covered much of the body. This was to protect them from the sun.

1 *Answers will vary. Suggested answers:* A drawing of people in the 1970s at the beach without a hat and a drawing of people in the 1990s wearing long sleeved swimming costumes.

Week 36, Day 3

Pg 194

1 Check for correct spelling of each word.

2 Missing letters are underlined

a fitness b enjoyment c softness d thickness e blackness f darkness

3 a payment b treatment c fairness d movement e amusement f amazement

4 a sadnes sadness b darknes darkness c amazment amazement

Week 36, Day 4

Pg 195

1 Check for correct spelling of each word.

2 a argument b punishment c equipment d excitement

3 a willingness b astonishment c entertainment

Week 36, Day 5

Pg 196

1 a thanks b won't c yeah d see ya e dunno f kid

2 a everybody b very good c delicious d would have e What is the matter? f quite soon

3 I have never been to Adelaide.

REVIEW 4

Spelling

Pg 197

1 Missing letters are underlined

a skate b smile c sheet d afraid

2 b

3 a happily b happiness c happiest

4 Missing letters are underlined

a saucer b dollar c finger d tractor

5 d

6 allways always

Grammar

Pg 198–199

1 a ate b drank c brought

2 a around b in

3 a with b in

4 a sat b dug

5 a She has lost her keys. b What are they doing?

6 *Answers will vary. Suggested answers:*

a Amy likes football because it is an action-packed game every week.

b Kate practised the flute while Nana read her new novel.

7 Becky has a white cat and Lucy has a black cat.

8 a anzac day, hobart b circular quay, manly

9 a Good morning b How are you?

Comprehension

200–201

1 b 2 a 3 d 4 a 5 d 6 a 7 b 8 d 9 b 10 c

WELL DONE!

This is to certify

---

has completed the

ABC Reading Eggspress

Year 2

program.

Date

Signature

ABC Reading Eggs Reading Skills for Year 2

www.readingeggs.com.au

ISBN: 978-1-74215-510-4

Reprinted 2023, 2024, 2025
Distributed by:
Pascal Press,
PO Box 250,
Glebe NSW 2037

Written by Laura Anderson
Publisher: Katy Pike
Editors: Kate Mihaljek, Amy Russo and Amanda Santamaria
Design and layout by Modern Art Production Group
Printed in China by 1010 Printing International Ltd